The Con

Also By Alistair Boyle

The Missing Link

The Con

A GIL YATES PRIVATE INVESTIGATOR NOVEL

By Alistair Boyle

Allen A. Knoll, Publishers
Santa Barbara, CA

Library of Congress Cataloging-in-Publication Data

Boyle, Alistair.
    The con : a Gil Yates private investigator novel / by Alistair
Boyle. --1st ed.
        p. cm.
    ISBN 0-9627297-9-5 (alk. paper)
    I. Title.
PS3552.0917C66   1996
813' .54--dc20   95-52375
                                                                          CIP

*Cover art: Claude Monet (1840-1926) "Rue Montorgueil" 1878.
Oil. 24.2 x 12.9 inches.*

*Text Typeface is ITC Galliard, 11 point
Printed on 60-pound Lakewood white, acid-free paper
Case bound with Kivar 9, Smyth Sewn*

1

I have always had a soft spot in my heart for a con man. I'm not sure why. He is usually a man (sorry, ladies, most of them seem to be men) who makes his living outsmarting those who are smarter than he is.

He usually plays on the greed and the get-rich-without-working nature of people who have had more education and advantages than he had. People who should know better.

So looking for the most successful and most elusive con man was an assignment I couldn't resist.

The call came from the big man himself, Franklin d'Lacy. There was no baloney with an intermediary secretary. No executive wait while the honcho cleared his throat.

"Mr. Yates," he spoke clearly, distinctly into my voice mail at the phone company, with a clipped diction that put you in mind of the British Empire. It was only an affectation, though a very good one. "Your services have been recommended to me by a member of our board, and I would appreciate a return phone call at your earliest convenience. I understand you are most discreet, and in this matter, that will be a prerequisite. Please tell no one of this call. You may reach me at this number during business hours. Mine begin at seven. It is my private line. Should someone else pick up the phone, hang up. I will always identify myself by saying, 'Franklin d'Lacy,' when I answer the phone."

Wow. Franklin d'Lacy, high-profile managing director of our Los Angeles Metropolitan Museum of Art.

I really hadn't planned on taking a second case. It was a fluke I got a first case. A lark. I didn't even have a license. In fact, I paid a $5,000 fine for not having one—but when you get a $250,000 fee, $5,000 is, as they say, pistachios. Or something like that. For while I am a well-read guy and I can quote verbatim from Shakespeare, the King James' Bible, Chaucer, Stephen Vincent Benét, and a hostess of others, you name it, clichés never seem to stick with me. Not in the right form, at any rate.

Of course, that quarter-million fee was shrunk somewhat. First and forestalled by the lovely folks at the Internal Revenue Service, in conjunction with what is charmingly referred to here at home as the California Franchise Tax Board. They knocked off something like a hundred grand, which conclusively demonstrates they are able to turn a dollar a lot easier than I can. But heck, almost anybody has been able to turn a dollar easier than I. When you work for your father-in-law, as I do, you take the crumbs.

So after taxes and doling out honorariums to those who helped me get my fee, and paying my expenses, including a loan from Daddybucks, my dauntless father-in-law, I had around a hundred grand stashed in a secret bank account—and, as they say down at the Federal Reserve Board, that's nothing to cough at.

Of course, you wouldn't expect me to deprive myself of the vegetables of my labor, so I picked up a bauble or two, in the form of some specimen exotic palms, as well as some hummingbird dingers of cycads—hundreds of years old. I got quite a bargain with the cycads, the most expensive, *Encephalartos woodii*, costing a mere six grand, which just happens to be more disposable income than I've made in my entire life. Daddybucks has always seen to it that my disposable income is minimal, while funneling the big disposable bucks to my charming wife, Dorcas, who I affectionately call Tyranny Rex—but not to her face.

Dorcas is a glass blower who makes adorable figurines that she sells at a fraction of their cost—when she's lucky. Together you could say we have two grown children—if you weren't too literal about it.

You might wonder how I could sneak those expensive plants by the vulture eye of my wife without the second degree on where I got the bucks for such a purchase. But Tyranny Rex doesn't know cycads from Swiss cheese, and she rarely ventures out of the garage, where she blows her glass. She has, as they say, the lungs for it.

When I say I have half a mind to do something, my wife says I am being overly optimistic—but, no matter, I did have half a brain to let this potential job pass. But there is no feeling like the feeling of being needed.

Besides, what can you lose returning a phone call? Quite a lot, actually, but I put in a call to Franklin d'Lacy, managing director of the Los Angeles Metropolitan Museum of Art.

In that clipped British put-on voice, he invited me to his office for a chat. It was, to me, like an invitation to chat with Clint Eastwood or the President of the U.S., whatever his name is, for Franklin d'Lacy is known the world under for his flamboyant acquisitions, from pre-Columbian baskets to African masks to Grecian urns to Renaissance paintings and back again. Every move Franklin d'Lacy made was well-documented in the media. Just the hint of his presence would send the newshounds to the three winds, hoping against hope he would make some newsworthy faux pas or otherwise fall into some scandal. Whatever he did, he was good copy, and he knew it.

I always thought a museum was a good place to go if the library was closed. Stare palaces, I call them. You go to stare at a bunch of objects with a lot of other people who stare decisively. After a while you are stared out, with about half the museum to go. You stare your way to the end with less appreciation and possibly no absorption, but you don't leave without some sense of accomplishment at having "done" the museum. Conveniently, these repositories of "art" exist in virtually every hamlet worth its sugar, so you can stare with the fervent hope of uplift wherever you go.

I liked portraits best—the closest thing to characterizations in books, I guess. I was not partial to deer hanging by their feet with their throats slit, nor to roast pigs with apples in their mouths. And contemporarily I thought Minimalist art a good joke on all the starers. A couple strands of string on a nail on the wall, a straight neon tube, single-color canvases, all left me chilly.

The Los Angeles Metropolitan Museum of Art (LAMMA, as in lamma beans—we have a real fetish for acronyms in this throat of the woods) had what Franklin d'Lacy, director and curator, never tired of calling "an eclectic mix".

I was invited into the inner sanctum by a spiffy-looking secretary in heels that might have well served the fire department hook-and-ladder troops. The heels were the ladders, she was the hook.

It was through that eclectic mix that I was now wending, concentrating my stares on the secretary who was leading the way. The door on the first floor said:

MUSEUM OFFICES

With the polished door closed behind me, the quiet of the eclectic mix was behind me. I was in a vital office with a dozen polished chrome-and-formica desks, and boys and girls, dressed for important matters, were crawling all over the place, like bees engaged in the production of honey.

Franklin d'Lacy had a reputation for running a chaotic ship. But his ship was a pleasant ship—plywood wall, laminated with Brazilian rosewood, and *objets d'art* all over the place. Museums were like icebergs, with ninety-five percent of the stash hidden below stairs. It would be a sin in a museum to suffer bare walls. Not here. There was more eclectic mix here with the peons. I mumbled my name, connected to that of Franklin d'Lacy.

d'Lacy was all smiles as he rose to greet me. "So good of you to come, Yates," he beamed. I could see in a flash why he was so good at raising bucks for his museum.

(He always referred to it as "my museum". It didn't win him any extra friends.)

He was the quintessential salesman, but way too suave for used cars. High-end real estate, maybe, or mainframe computers.

He struck me as a guy sensitive of his height, but he wasn't that short. At five foot, eleven-some inches I was taller, but only by a couple of inches. He was dressed in one of those banker, pin-stripe, Brooks Brothers worsteds.

He was tan, had enough hair for the whole board of directors and was fit as a cello. Did some jogging in the early morning to get the juices flowing, and after work a couple nights a week worked out those juices on a personal trainer of whom, it was said, he had carnal knowledge.

"Hold the calls, Miss Craig," he said, as the young woman backed out of the room. Do you suppose she sensed my predilection to stare at her sculptured buns? Everything here was a work of art—so much to stare at. The staff, I decided, was selected for their stare appeal, just like Hammurabi's nickels and dimes and Titian's oils.

So you could tell pin-stripe d'Lacy from your run-of-the-mill banker, he wore a gardenia in his jacket buttonhole. I could smell it from where I sat across his Brazilian rosewood desk, which was the genuine article, not the laminate, and was, roughly, the size of Brazil.

I couldn't get over how darn gracious he was. "Are you comfortable in that chair? May I get you something to drink?"

"Thanks, I'm fine."

"Well," he said, taking his measure of me down a nose that could have held its own with the marble statues in the foyer, "Michael Hadaad speaks very highly of you."

I almost fell off my chair. Michael Hadaad? The same guy who tried to clean out my sinuses with a bullet rather than turn over my fee after I had accomplished his goal? He was the last guy in the world I would expect to recommend me.

Michael Hadaad is my pseudonym for this slightly

tarnished megabucks who put me through loops on my first case, from which I was grateful to escape with my skin.

d'Lacy seemed amused at my reaction. He was looking at me over the little temple he had made with his manicured fingertips. I could tell he wanted in the worst way to be British. It represented class to him.

"Michael is on our board, you know," he said.

"No, I..."

"Given us a nice piece of change over the years, I daresay."

I nodded. Why else would that creep be on LAMMA's board of directors?

"Of course, he said you were a rank amateur. 'Childish,' was, I believe, the way he put it. 'A wimp, impossible to reason with'..."

"So why...?"

"Why is obvious, isn't it? You solved his problem. Look here, Yates, I'm a results-oriented guy. I wouldn't have made my museum a world-class institution if I hadn't been. Why, I'd work with a wooden-legged centipede if he brought me the pigeon."

Was there, I wondered, buried in there, flattery?

"He also told me the most remarkable thing about you," he said.

"Oh?"

Franklin d'Lacy nodded. "Said you worked exclusively on a contingency basis." He was especially amused when he said, "Michael quoted you as saying a thousand a day and expenses was tacky."

"Well, perhaps I..."

"That's what interests me," d'Lacy said. "That, and the fact that Michael assures me you are an absolute nut for privacy and secrecy. Discretion, he says, is your byword. No business cards, no office, not even," this he pronounced with relish, "a license."

Was Franklin d'Lacy really winking at me?

"Of course, I understand a contingency fee comes a lot higher than I could buy one of those small-timers, but if you achieve my goal, I will pay you one million dollars."

I sank back in the chrome-and-black-leather chair. My head was spinning—only my second job and I didn't have to go through the fee litany—he offered me more than I'd ever dare ask.

"You're not asking anything illegal?" I eyed him warily. My father told me there were no golden apples, and I've never had the slightest reason to doubt him.

"*Au contraire,*" he said in elegant French. Though for some reason it would not have surprised me to learn that those were his only two words in the Gallic language. "What you will be doing is countering an illegal activity. We've been defrauded; conned, if you will." He stopped abruptly and up came the manicured temple again, and this time his pink lips kissed his fingers ever so lightly. "To proceed further, I will need your assurance that what I say is to be held in the strictest confidence, even if you do not want the job. I would, of course, appreciate your indication of willingness to undertake the task, should you find it to your liking."

"It is difficult to commit without a full understanding of what you want accomplished," I said. "It's possible what you want is beyond my experience. That doesn't mean I would refuse to tackle it, but rather that you must make the choice." I'd already subtracted the taxes from the million and figured I ought to clear six hundred grand, easy. Of course, with what he told me, I knew it wouldn't be that easy.

"The secrecy," I avowed, "goes without saying. I speak to no one about my cases. I tell no one about conversations with my principal."

"But if you don't take the job, I'm not your principal."

"To me, you are, the moment you utter one confidential word. But are you sure you need this secrecy? It can be a hindrance, you know."

He nodded. Then he laid out his story. He needed the secrecy.

2

Franklin d'Lacy was warming to his subject. He was, they said, a consummate actor, and I was flattered at his obvious efforts in my behalf. There was nothing unpleasant about being an audience when there was a million dollars in the cat.

A quick perusal of his surroundings made me wonder how much all the junk was worth. There were those svelte white box stands with *objets* on top that looked like they were some Indian (aka Native American) castoffs. Stuff that I always imagined was abandoned in a cave somewhere by an ancient "artist" who sold the good stuff to his leader to bury with him.

On d'Lacy's walls were Impressionist paintings that looked better to me than the stuff in Stare City. But, heck, you had to keep the stuff rotating, and it was lots better hanging it in the director's office than it was burying it in the vaults.

It all contributed to the feeling I got sitting among these treasures, that this was some big-shot guy who could work amid zillions of bucks' worth of art—a lot more than the C.E.O. of the biggest companies could.

Franklin d'Lacy had a faraway look in his eyes—as though he hadn't quite decided to confide in me. It didn't take long for me to get uncomfortable. I shifted in my chrome-and-black-leather chair and he looked startled, as though he had forgotten I was there. "Oh, Yates," he said,

"I'm sorry. Reverie," he added with a sigh. "I was just reliving the horror of it all."

"So what happened?"

He spread out his hands over the desk. "I was conned," he said. "Pure and simple. And I should be the last person in the world to be taken in by an art con."

"It was someone you trusted?"

"Impeccable credentials," he nodded. "Known him for years."

"What happened?"

"He pulled a switcheroo," he said, "pure and simple."

"Forgive me," I said, "but how does one of these 'switcheroos' work?"

He shook his head and ran his hand from his forehead to his neck. "I was so *stupid*!" he groaned. "Please forgive me," he said. "I can't talk about it—or even *think* about the scam without my flesh crawling." At last he met my eyes. "I heard through that granddaddy of intelligence, the grapevine, that a missing Monet had been located, and might be for sale. Okay, all the antennae shoot up right away. Fraud! Forgery! Fake—the three 'F's. There's another 'F' that stands for what happened to me, but we can talk about that later. And, of course, everyone knows that things that seem too good to be true, usually are. So I was plenty skeptical. But I knew the dealer who had the work. Impeccable reputation. So I called him."

"Where was he?"

"London," he said, wincing at the memory. "He was a man of peerless pedigree, with a simply spotless reputation. I can assure you, no one in the art world would have ever questioned his integrity or his judgment."

"So you took his word on the authenticity of this Monet painting?"

He looked at me as though I were crazy. "Of course not. Do you take me for a fool? No one spends that kind of money on faith."

"What kind of money?"

"Sixteen million," he muttered so it sounded like he would rather have said "thousand."

I whistled.

"Yes," he said, "but it was a knockdown price. I know the Getty would have paid two, three million more. This was a painting to kill for. Who knows, at auction, with the frenzy of bidding, it could have fetched double what we paid."

"So why didn't they auction it?"

"Recession," he shrugged his shoulders. It was almost a question. "We're in an art recession. It's chancy. You can't be sure what you'll get. Prices are depressed. Fifty-million-dollar Van Goghs we will not see again for a while. So they would have been taking the chance that the painting would pull that much. If it didn't, they feared a stigma would glom onto it and it could be years till it regained its value. Hey, I asked all those questions too, but now isn't it obvious why they didn't auction it? Even to you?"

There was something about the way he said those last three words that didn't engender a feeling that he had a significant appreciation of my talents. So as not to disillusion him, I shook my head stupidly, and he picked up the ball for a touchdown.

"They swindled me! They sold me the picture, got the money, and kept the picture. It is a con that would have been tougher to bring off with an auction house. They have to possess the work before it goes on the block."

"So how did it work?" I asked. "Logistically?"

"I went to London to see the painting, of course," he said. He was talking to a naif again. I didn't mind. Rather get too much information than too little. "It was the genuine article, all right. My eyes almost fell out of my head on the spot. I knew it was worth more than they were asking, which made me suspicious of its provenance."

"Provenance?"

"Its history. Who owned it—the chain of title from the painter till today."

"And?"

"It was believable—but I'll tell you, looking at that painting I was willing to believe anything."

"Was it a forgery?"

"Oh, no. Not that one. That was the genuine article."

"How do you know?"

Franklin d'Lacy threw up his hands at the effrontery he must have felt having his expertise doubted by a babe in the forest. "It's my specialty—Impressionism. It was my thesis—Monet is my favorite. I know his work like the back of my hand."

"But the painting you got was not the same one?"

He nodded, wearily.

"Is it customary to pay in advance?"

"I wouldn't say customary. But it's not that unusual. Especially in these private sales. No auction house or gallery will send out a painting without having the money in hand."

"So what recourse do you have?"

"That is the question of the hour. Reputation in this business is everything. I can tell you, this man—my dealer in London—would not sacrifice his reputation for twice this amount."

"What does he say?" I asked.

"Nothing."

"Nothing? He must have some answer."

"Nothing. He's disappeared."

"Ran off with your money?"

He looked at me, his eyes bleary. "Try as I might to imagine that about him, I simply cannot. About a dozen other dealers I know, but not Jacques Moran. As Sam Goldwyn used to say, 'In two words—im-possible.'"

"Foul play?"

"What else?"

"So what do you think happened?"

"I think someone got to the shipment somewhere. Here, there, en route, and substituted this forgery."

"When did you see the real item last?"

"I saw it being crated in the basement of the Moran

Gallery on New Bond Street, London, England."

"How did it get to you?"

"A truck picked it up and drove it to the airport, where it was flown to Los Angeles. Our customs broker saw it through customs and delivered it here."

"Was it in the same box you saw it packed in?"

"Yes."

"Do you still have the box?"

He nodded.

"May I see it?"

"Certainly. I'll take you to it myself—if we come to an understanding." He looked so forlorn, I was ready to agree to anything he wanted.

"Have you gone to the police?" I asked.

"Oh, no," he answered quickly.

"Isn't that required to collect on the insurance?"

He drew in a heavy draught of air. "I don't want the insurance money," he said through painfully clenched teeth, "I want the painting. Do you realize what this could do to me—to my reputation, my career?"

"No, I don't," I said, puzzled at his disparate gloom. "You acted in good faith."

"But don't you see how it looks? It looks like I paid sixteen million for a forgery."

"Is it a good forgery?"

"No, it is *not*!" he said. "To add insult to injury. As if *I* could have bought *that* painting!"

"Maybe you are unduly worried about your reputation. Your story is certainly plausible. The people who count will believe you. I really think the police here and in London would satisfy you."

He shook his head. "It's no secret that some of the public, the board even, don't like my style. Too flamboyant, they say. What they mean is I am a popularizer—bringing art to the attention of the masses, when everybody knows it is meant exclusively for the aristocracy." He arched an eyebrow to emphasize what an arch idea that was.

"Sometimes I think they would be more comfortable

12

with a Ph.D. in tweeds. You know, the type who sucks on a pipe and sucks up to everybody at the same time; who nods his approval and treads water until pension time. There's no doubt about it, a small but tenacious faction here would love nothing better than to see me fall on my face."

"I see."

"I don't mind telling you we are always being compared to New York—and always unfavorably. This picture would have made those smug New Yorkers rear up on their hind legs and take notice." He pursed his lips and shook his head. "With this news in the public domain, they'd just have a field day."

"But it seems you have a terrible time constraint. How long will it be before there is a clamoring to see the work? Until someone doubts its authenticity?"

"Exactly. The purchase has been a secret thus far, with only the acquisition committee in on it. But they all have friends. They're bound to say something, and before you know it we'll be tripping over television cables."

"How many on the committee?"

"Acquisitions? Five."

"Who are they?"

"Myself, Michael Hadaad, Emma Thornsen, Sam Bisbing and Karl Graul."

"Could any of them tell it was a forgery?"

"Sure."

"Without having seen the original?"

"Graul, maybe. Not the others. Hadaad knows, of course."

"Is there any need to tell the others?"

"Eventually. I haven't said anything, of course. So mum has got to be the word here. And your discretion comes highly recommended. I hope we can keep the lid on this thing until you find the right painting."

"You're sure it exists?"

"Of course I'm sure. I saw it with my own eyes."

"You're sure you couldn't have been fooled?" It was an ego-testing question and touchy. I knew it, just after I asked.

He had the perfect answer. "Of course I can be fooled. And I have been. But I can't be fooled this easily. Apparently someone thought I could be. But when you see the genuine article in the flesh, so to speak, then two weeks later are presented with a forgery, even if it *were* a good one, why, I daresay even *you* would know the difference."

I wondered if I should thank him for that vote of confidence. I said, "Hm," instead. There was no mistaking d'Lacy's good opinion of himself. I guessed in his line of work there was no option.

"Well," he said, the weight of the world seemed to be crushing him, "you think you can find the painting and bring it back to me?"

There it was. How could anyone answer that cavalierly in the affirmative? "How much can you give me to go on?"

He looked shocked. "I thought you only got paid if you got results."

"That's true. Though in this case it could be a real long shot. What I meant was, what hard information can you give me to begin? I have the name of the dealer, Jacques Moran, New Bond Street, London.

He could supply me with a picture of Moran. Franklin was in it too. It was taken, he said, outside Moran's gallery in London, just after the deal was made. Both men were smiling, but I decided, perhaps unfairly, that Moran's was the broader smile.

I asked for a letter of introduction to his acquaintances in the art world and he wrote it out long hand. He explained that he didn't want anyone, even his secretary, to know what we were doing.

I was on the verge of asking him for a little pocket money to traipse to Europe, when he said, "Shall I write you a note concerning our agreement?"

"I think that might be a good idea," I said.

"Of course, you get your hands on a sixteen-million-dollar painting, I don't think you'd ever have much trouble getting a million dollars for it. But it's best to have an agreement so we understand what's involved." He began writing. "A million dollars on delivery of the original Monet described in the bill of sale—a copy of which I'm providing. No advances, no draws, no obligation unless the painting is delivered."

"I take it you have photographs of the original work?"

"I do indeed, and I shall supply you with several." He opened his middle desk drawer and rifled through a stack of photos and picked out three for me.

"May I compare these to the forgery?"

He nodded.

It wasn't much to go on. The name and last-known address of a missing man.

"Who are some of the great forgers in the world?" I asked.

"For this kind of art, there is really only one master forger. That's Albert Durant. He's well known—he's almost a cult figure."

"Could he have done this forgery?"

"No way. He'd be insulted at the thought. This is so amateurish."

"Any idea of guys who could have done this?"

"Or gals. There are thousands of them. Any half-decent art student could have turned out this fake."

"Any idea where Durant is?"

He shook his head. "May still be in jail for all I know."

"Where was that?"

"Europe someplace."

He took me to the basement, where the forgery was stored in a vault—still in the packing crate. It was about two feet by three feet.

"It looks like the crate was opened several times," I observed.

"But that's not unusual," he said. "Customs often inspect these boxes, then seals them up again."

I compared the Monet in the photograph to the

forgery in the box. I had trouble telling the difference.

"You see the difference?" Franklin d'Lacy asked.

"I can't say I do—yet."

"Look at the brushwork. That's where a forger is bound to fall down. Brushwork is like fingerprints, very difficult to forge."

"It's also hard to see in the photograph," I said.

"Yes," he conceded.

"But you said even I could tell it was a forgery."

"Yes, if you saw the original, then saw this. Why, look at it, doesn't even the paint look suspiciously new?"

"Hm," I pondered. "I suppose, some..."

"Well, if you had a trained eye, I'm sure you'd see it."

"Do you have photos of this painting?"

"Yes."

"May I have a couple of those?"

"What good will that do you?"

"I might more readily see the difference."

"I doubt it, but I'll certainly give you some."

"I'm just wondering, if I can't tell from this, how am I going to know if I found the real one?"

"You'll know," he said. "It sparkles."

3

My gracious host, Franklin d'Lacy, took me back upstairs after locking the vault and gave me pictures of the forgery. Comparing them to the pictures of the "original," I still couldn't discern the difference.

"Aren't you afraid someone on the staff will get into that vault and blow the horn?" I asked him.

"I have the only key," he smiled. "It's on my key chain, and we are never parted."

I left him, promising to ponder the job for twenty-four hours and call him then.

On the surface it seemed like a great kick in the pantaloons to take it on—but the more I thought about it, the more impossible it seemed. When people disappear, it is generally for one of two reasons. One, they want to hide, or two, someone else wants them out of circulation, perhaps permanently. Either way, someone has a great stock in keeping your prey out of sight. What is one guy against that?

On the other hand, the art world in the sixteen-million-buck stratosphere must be a fairly limited sphere. And maybe it could be cracked.

Then there was the time pressure. How long would it be until word got out that the highest profile museum director in the world had been swindled? I mused I could probably get a million dollars for that information alone.

It was, I should be embarrassed to admit, that million dollars that finally made up my mind.

I wanted it.

Money, I decided, was as good a motive for doing something as anything else.

Especially a lot of money.

***

Home, sweet home was not always sweet, but it was always home. A tract house in the flatlands of Torrance, California, at the foothills of the majestic hill that was Palos Verdes. My father-in-law lived in Palos Verdes. It is upscale and so is he.

We weren't too far from the Del Amo shopping center, which, for a time, had the distinction of being the largest shopping center in the world, until someone in the Midwest one-upped them.

Shopping centers to me were like museums. How much stuff could you stare at and for how long? You had to be in awfully good shape simply to walk from one end of Del Amo to the other, without looking left or right.

The thing that set our earth-tone tract house off from the others was my palm trees and cycads. For I am what is referred to in horticultural circles as a palm nut.

California tract houses usually sat on limited pieces of *terra fermata*. Ours was no exception. Over the years, my palm trees have taken more and more space, so now, from any side of the lot, you can barely see the house.

I always paused to admire my palms before I went into the house. It gave me a spiritual rejuvenation before facing my formidable wife, Tyrannosaurus Rex.

As soon as I opened the door, I was greeted with her characteristic "He's here, oh joy, oh rapture!" And it just dripped with sarcasm. This was usually followed with "You're late" (I hardly ever was) or "Where have you been?" But when I gave her a straight answer to this one, I noticed she wasn't listening. The walls were lined with glass shelves—the better to show off the glass figurines that adorned them, Dorcas decided. You could see under them, as well as over and straight on. And she had strip fluorescent lights installed on the wall to light the little darlings at night. As she would say, "Oh joy, oh rapture!"

It was my secret fantasy to one day take a baseball bat to the whole megillah. Like those prevalent scenes in movies where someone goes berserk and trashes a room. I haven't done it yet, of course, though I flatter myself that I have come close.

Tyranny Rex puts me in mind of one of those movie actors dressed up like a woman. It seems every decade or so the taste-making film makers decide it's time for another hilarious movie of some star in drag. Jack Lemmon, Tony Curtis, Dustin Hoffman and Robin Williams have all clomped across the silver screen in nylons and lipstick, and everyone falls on the floor laughing. Why is that, I wonder? Nobody laughs at all the women dressed up like men, in pants, jackets and neckties.

Anyway, those guys in drag put me in mind of Tyranny Rex. Actually, the Robin Williams one is uncanny. Of course I don't tell her. She wouldn't see the humor in it.

Nor do I argue with her anymore. I learned long ago a well-placed "Yes, dear" was more effective than the most flawlessly reasoned, unassailably logical point I could make.

Tyranny Rex's mind was on higher things than where I had been or why I was late. Her mind was on higher things than housework too. You couldn't say she was inept at housework, because she never tried it. Who knows, with a little effort she might have been a world-class dust buster.

For instance, three days ago she broke a glass jar that was sitting for a week on an ironing board that was begging for some utilization. The shards are still where they fell. Her comment to me was, "You don't go barefoot, do you?"

"Sometimes."

"Well, don't."

Tonight I am celebrating the third anniversary of the break with an 8 ½-by 11 inch paper on which I have placed a large "3" filling the page so someone with under-par eyesight wouldn't miss it. Tomorrow I shall change it to "4," and so on, until she deigns to clean it up.

Tonight, it turned out, Tyranny was in the garage blowing glass. That meant canned soup for dinner. Glass blowing is an occupation you might consider dangerous, and I confess, in the early years, I entertained the hope that she and the house would suddenly go down in smoke. But as time went on, I suppressed that desire. My palms and cycads were growing nicely and I didn't want them to burn.

The windowless garage was dark except for the floor lamp Tyranny had confiscated from the living room. It was throwing a circle of light on her work space, with its flame and her glass bars and pinchers. She wasn't blowing tonight, she was shaping.

Long ago I learned that with Tyranny the best approach was the most direct. Pussyfooting around didn't do diddly with her. Wham! Just hit her with it between the eyes and if it was outrageous enough, it got her attention. It made me empathetic to the cavemen who used to bash their women over the head. Not that I would ever think of doing such a thing to Tyranny Rex. Why, I wouldn't even dare to write about the thought, if I thought anyone was going to read it.

"Dorcas, dear..."

"Hm?" she made the sound but she didn't break her concentration on the glass rod on the flame. She was making one of her little boys urinating. I never understood her fascination with the subject. It was a big seller, she said. She never made girls urinating.

"I was thinking of taking a tour of Europe."

"Are you crazy?"

"Well, the kids are finally out of the house and we have some freedom—I've never been, you know."

"I've been a dozen times," she said as though she were weary of the whole business. "When would you go?"

"How does tomorrow sound?"

"Stupid," she said without missing a turn of the glass

bar. "My going with you at this time of year is out of the question. This weekend I have the sale at the mall. Next weekend I'm in San Diego."

I noticed she spoke with her usual finality. No negotiations were offered. No "Why don't we go in April instead?" One of the pitfalls of a long marriage might have been getting *too* comfortable—taking everyone and everything for granted. There was one person Tyranny Rex didn't take for granted.

"Have you asked Daddy Wemple if you can go?"

"Not yet," I said, piling on the diplomacy. "I wanted to clear it with you first."

"Clear it?" She hoisted her eyebrows. "Really?" Was that the beginning of a smile I saw on her face? "Well, of course I don't approve of rash and irresponsible actions, but I suppose you're entitled to a mid-life crisis. Not to say that your whole life hasn't been one long and uninterrupted mid-life crisis. Look at all those goddamn palms, for example. We live in a goddamn jungle, for God's sake."

Tyranny Rex liked to swear, but her profane vocabulary was sorely limited.

"How long were you planning on being gone?"

Neat the way she put that. Her perspective: being gone from here. Not "How long are you going for?"—that would be *my* perspective. The last thing she would consider.

"Oh, I don't know," I said, falling asleep I was so casual, "maybe a month or so."

"A month!" she exploded. She had the luxury of the explosion because she had finished pulling her urinating boy into shape and he was cooling. I would rather have had Tyranny cool, but that was a harder go.

"Well, it's a big place," I dissembled, "to see it properly..."

"But a month?"

It made me wonder what she would do with me in the subject month. We certainly didn't do much together in the last couple months. I decided it was control.

"Well, I could make it shorter if that would be better

for you," I heard myself say, though I was thinking something more aggressively unpleasant.

"You're such a loser," she muttered, and I realized that was the end of it. I didn't even have to say "Yes, dear." She actually didn't call me a loser, but rather the most reviled part of the anatomy. I've told her many times I don't like being called that, but it cuts no ice cubes with her. Perhaps she means it in an endearing sense, if that's possible.

While I ate my can of Campbell's clam chowder, Manhattan style, alone, for dinner, I remembered Tyranny Rex had not even asked me where I was getting the money for such a trip. There were, I decided, some advantages to being married to a woman who was so self-absorbed.

Daddybucks would be another kettle of chickens. Daddy Wemple, Tyranny called him. I called him Daddy Pimple or Daddybucks because he had both; not that she actually *heard* me call him that. At work some of us called him the Giant Thumb. He had such an enormous thumb that everyone in the place fit under it. He was a control freak, but in these twenty-some years I had learned a thing or two about how to get around that fat, omnipresent thumb.

This time, sitting on his raised platform which enabled him to see all the bodies in his operation, I wasn't doing so hot.

"What in hell are you *talking* about?" was his immediate response. I couldn't answer right away because I had trained myself that with Daddybucks, the world-master rhetorical questioner, self-evident answers were neither called for nor necessary. But as he just stared me down I began to think, this time he wanted an answer, and I didn't really have an answer to give. I couldn't really tell him what the hell I was talking about.

"Well, big mouth," I could say, "I'm off on a safari which, if successful, will give me a million smugolies, about six hundred fat ones after taxes, at which point all you'll see of me is my back." That, of course, is what I wanted to say. But there was always the chance, considerable in this

22

instance, that it wouldn't skillet out so easily and I would be crawling back to beg for my meager livelihood.

Instead, I said, "Dorcas has been with you and your missus five times." Surprising myself at the use of "missus," which Daddybucks Wemple uses all the time, but which I abhor. "I've never been to Europe. Not getting any younger, I guess. Kids are gone." I was pretty well mumbling by this time, when I noticed him winking at me.

Startled by his sudden informality, I pinched my eyes shut to see if he were still in that stance when I opened them.

He was even better; he slammed his meaty paw down on his desk and said, "By God, Malvin, (I was Malvin Stark in the real world) I underestimated you. Europe? Paris! London! Rome! I'll bet she's a real looker."

"She?" I muttered, swallowing the word with my surprise.

"Well, man, nobody expects a stud like you to travel alone."

There it was. He was making fun of me. He realized how ridiculous it was to suppose that a guy like me could attract a young, attractive girl. I couldn't argue, so I didn't. I played right into his hands. He winked again.

"Hell," he said, "have a grand time. We won't even miss you around here. I always told Dorcas I was doing her a favor keeping you on the payroll; why, a half-decent secretary could do your work on her lunch hour."

I was too dumbfounded to speak. He seemed to be coming down on my side anyway, what were a few insults?

"God in heaven, to be footloose and fancy-free again." He shook his head, marveling, it seemed, at my good fortune. "Go to it, Malvin. Take a lot of pictures. I imagine a guy like you would take a lot of pictures, don't you?"

"Don't know," I shrugged. "Never been there."

"Aw, take my advice, leave the camera at home. Gets in the way of your enjoyment, and you never look at the pictures anyway. And besides that, the postcard people take better pictures."

"Thanks," I said, "I..."

He waved me off with the same hand that had pounded the desk. "Don't mention it," and he winked again with eyes as big as Luxembourg.

4

My fear of flying has no rational basis. I have seen reams of impressive statistics showing driving is thirty-two times more dangerous than flying—but I am driving the car. I am not relying on the skill and alertness of some faceless automaton in a uniform. The milkman used to wear a uniform. The postman wears a uniform. Would you get in a plane if he were in the cockpit? At least you know what the postman looks like.

After coldly analyzing all the rational reasons why flying is the safest way to travel, I still have the fear.

Flying just isn't natural unless you happen to be a bird. I'll never understand how a thing as big as a plane that holds four hundred people and their tons of luggage can stay up in the sky. Look at the trouble the Wright brothers had. And the Kittyhawk thing was a feather next to these jumbo jets.

So, the infrequent occasions I am called upon to fly, I, in turn, call upon the Deity to hold the sucker up.

Now, if I were flying alone, I would be fairly comfortable in that request because, being something of a self-confessed wimp, I am not this big sinner or anything. Not the kind of guy who would tick off the Big Mother in the sky. *Or* Her husband. But when you are dealing with a whole planeload of strangers, there are bound to be one or two at least who have aggravated the Big Boss big time— enough to knock a flimsy, overweight hunk of metal out of the sky any day of the week. I mean, we are talking about a personage who turned Lot's wife into a pillar of salt because she turned around. Next to that, dropping a plane would be child's play.

I have not mentioned this to anyone before and would appreciate it not being blabbed around. I do my best to look like a macho hunk getting on and off planes because I see no option in this line of work, but that's on the outside. Inside, my entrails are jelly. And if you can picture how jelly would hold up in an earthquake, you can get some idea how I feel flying.

As if that were not enough torture, I have a fetish for finding the rock-bottom fare to anywhere. This time I hooked up with an outfit with Virgin in their name. Since this word connotes lack of experience, it seems a weird name for an airline. But price is price and the plane was anything but a virgin. Springs were poking through the seats in such a manner that could compromise one's constitutional right of privacy, legroom had continually shrunk to the point where you could only sit comfortably if you had no legs, and the food would be rejected by any self-respecting garbage disposal.

But the most nefarious saving had to be economizing on the amount of fresh air pumped into the cabin. Air, like water, is free (as in, "The best things in life are free"), but pumping them costs. So along with my prayer for a safe flight (God should keep a good grip on the plane so it wouldn't fall out of the sky), I said one to immunize me against influenza, diphtheria, scarlet fever, bronchitis and whooping cough; or anything else you could pick up through stale air.

And once they closed the door you were in the bouillabaisse. Your breathing days were over.

To distract me from my concerns about the seaworthiness of the aircraft should we land in the sea, as in all probability we would, I brought every publication I could get my hands on that had to do with art forgery; Impressionist painting and Franklin d'Lacy.

The flight attendant, female from the best evidence, was prattling on about the safety features of the so-called aircraft and giving us inside tips on saving our lives "in the unlikely event of..." I wasn't listening. I didn't want anything to interfere with my panic.

When the plane leveled off and the rattling subsided somewhat, I was able to open my eyes and open the book on my lap. It was by the master art forger Albert Durant, the man Franklin d'Lacy mentioned as the best living forger. It was written in Durant's jail cell in his spare time and might have been subtitled "How to Forge Impressionist Paintings for Fun and Profit in Your Spare Time."

He was the quintessential con man, and reading his book I was surprised to find I was rooting for him every step of the way. He fooled people with his art, people who passed themselves off as experts, connoisseurs; curators and museum heads. He hadn't fooled Franklin d'Lacy, and that boosted d'Lacy in my estimation.

But this Durant guy, this great forger, could paint like any old master, from Rembrandt to Picasso, and hardly anyone could tell the difference. And he sold his forgeries for millions. But he couldn't give away his originals. To get out of jail he had to promise to stop forging paintings. And Franklin d'Lacy was left holding a forgery he said was too poor to have been done by Durant. That threatened not only acute embarrassment, but could cost him his job—and *his* museum sixteen million. A fine kettle of clams.

I turned next to d'Lacy's writings. As I opened the magazine to d'Lacy's opus I got a sudden blast of kerosene fuel. Flying by price has its costs.

It was a little hard to concentrate on d'Lacy's "scholarly" articles because the guy next to me had a fetish for using the telephone. "How are things going internationally?" he would ask, and, after a short pause, we were in for a rollicking round of statistics (he called them "stats") and humdrum blather about economic stimulants, recessionary spending and delights of that ilk.

It made me think if we could just legalize art forgery

we might get a lot more bucks, Deutsche marks, and yen into the economy.

After about twenty minutes, Gabby wore down. Maybe he realized what this airborne conversation was costing him; maybe he ran out of stats. As soon as he laid the phone to rest, I started reading "The Contemporary Appeal of Impressionist Painting," by Franklin d'Lacy, curator of Impressionist painting at the Houston Museum (before he came to L.A.). It appeared in one of these glitzy coffee-table magazines you bought for the pictures.

In d'Lacy's piece there were feints at the intrinsic value of the art itself, but mostly we were talking big-bucks museum acquisitions, auction prices then and now, and scarcity and demand out of some economic-theory primer. The bum rap wasn't that bum. d'Lacy *was* an art popularizer.

The article didn't give me much insight. I often wondered how one could tell the genuine art from the mock. In palms and cycads, it was easy. Plastic palm trees were nothing like the real McDougal. But d'Lacy wrote as an expert. Not a man who could be fooled.

I began to wonder if it was possible that he *was* fooled and he really got the painting he saw in London, but later realized, for some reason, it was suspect. Perhaps a colleague cast doubt; perhaps he received a tip.

When you think of someone paying sixteen million for a work of art it gives you a lot of food for speculation. What makes anything worth sixteen million dollars? It certainly isn't the thing itself. I read that the Japanese company that paid fifty-two million and change for the Van Gogh lost about $125,000 a day in interest on that money—so it was costing them $125,000 a day to look at that painting.

My thoughts turned from kerosene fuel and errant seat springs to Michael Hadaad. The guy who tried to sandwich a bullet between my sinuses. Hadaad was a guy who smelled worse than kerosene and was always poking you. He was my idea of a criminal, yet here he was, on the board of directors of one of the nation's leading art museums. And to have him recommend me for this job just blows me astray.

But, I suppose they were in a fix. Hadaad was probably banking on my naiveté in the affairs of the socially elite who run museums. Having him on the board is proof positive that members are picked for the size of their bankrolls. He doesn't even live *near* Los Angeles and I'm sure wouldn't know an Impressionist forgery if it fell on him labeled with six-inch block letters:

FORGERY

And yet here he was, an intimate of Herr Direktor, the great, beleaguered Franklin d'Lacy, who seemed an erudite and cultured guy. Hadaad was a bum with bucks. What possibly could d'Lacy see in him?

Okay, he probably laid millions on the museum; with each crooked arms sale he upped his ante to buy respectability. You could say if politics made strange bed partners, the art world was one big bawdyhouse.

Remember Ivan Boesky? Made hundreds of millions fraudulently. Sat on the boards of everything worth sitting on in New York, including the Metropolitan Museum of Art. They loved him and his money until the scandal went public, then goodbye, Ivan. Apparently Michael Hadaad was a small-time crook with big-time bucks.

The flight attendant came by to offer me something from a can. She was having big trouble with her contact lenses, and her lashes, heavily laden with mascara, were fluttering to beat the orchestra. I had a hunch she had been Miss Budweiser in the doldrums of prohibition.

I took the orange juice even though I realized all that was left of that poor orange was a semblance of its color. As I sipped my drink, where some carcinogenic food coloring had been substituted for vitamin C, I tried to get a handle on my situation.

How to ingratiate myself into the circles where paintings went for sixteen million a pop was not going to be a snap or a crackle for me. My appearance, though presentable, neat and clean, had not heretofore inspired any of

29

these high rollers to consider me one of them. I was a guy who looked like he didn't have two thousand-dollar bills to rub together.

It is not unusual to be out of your depth in an area where your depth is about an inch and a half.

As the flying Rube Goldberg made his descent, I turned the color of the mock orange drink. The yellow ingredient was from my fear of flying, the red from my terror at what I had gotten myself into.

My motto has always been: when in doubt, hum it by ear—and I was humming like crazy. Sometimes all that humming can get you in trouble if you are tone deaf.

5

My kerosene burner landed in the pitch black. I had shot a night's sleep plotting my strategy.

First, I would check into my flea-box hotel and conk out for a couple hours. Nothing was open at five in the morning anyway.

The night clerk at the Prince of Wales was a man of prodigious good humor who took delight in calling me "mate."

"Here's your key, mate. You'll find your room just at the top of the stairs, mate. Three flights up, mate. The staff at the Prince of Wales wishes you a most pleasant stay, mate, but don't look for a personal appearance of the Prince himself. He's been rather occupied of late, what with the tabloids kicking up such a fuss."

The prodigious smile on his ruddy face led me to believe he thought that terribly funny—mate.

You might think that a guy sitting with circa a hundred grand in a bank account completely unknown to his distaff and his boss father-in-law would blow himself to more lavish accommodations.

Well, I considered it, but several factors conspired against it: One, you can't teach an old cat new tricks. Once a skinflint by necessity, always a skinflint by habit. Two, this could wind up being a costly gig. Blowing the bankroll too early could be fatal. Three, a low profile is always judicious. Too much splash attracts suspicion. And last, but most cherished, I wanted to keep a nut to buy some more rare and exotic palms and cycads.

So I schlepped my suitcase up the three floors. My new mate at the desk didn't offer to help. Not his line, I supposed. He was sort of a toastmaster-greeter for the establishment (not blessed with one of those colorful medallions that said, "Hoteliers to Her Majesty the Queen." Carrying suitcases was not his bag.

It took a little finagling the key to get it to turn the lock. But the prospect of six more flights, round trip, encouraged me to persevere, and I got the door open.

It was a mixed blessing.

There was a rumpled bed and a formerly stuffed chair in the room. If there was something else, I missed it. The chair reminded me of the losing turkey in a Thanksgiving tussle. It had the stuffing kicked out of it.

The bed looked like it had been slept in. Well, perhaps "slept" is not the right word. I had booked myself into one of those hotbed operations where they rented rooms by the hour.

I was too tired to do the six flights round trip in the vain hope of getting a better "situation." So I dusted off the sheets with my hand, as though that would sterilize anything communicable, and I lay down in my clothes (further insulation from VD) on the edge of the bed on a portion of the sheet I estimated had been mainly unused.

I awoke to the first light, looked at my watch on the bedside table and realized no art galleries would be open at that hour and went back to sleep while I was thinking about it.

It was around ten a.m., London time, when I finally rolled out of bed. I had missed the complimentary continental breakfast, but my pal at the desk, who must have worked a twenty-four-hour shift, rustled up an old roll and some hot tea for me. "Glad to do it for you, mate."

Then he gave me the lowdown on the underground, and before you could say "New Bond Street," I was there.

The Jacques Moran Gallery was an understated hole

in the wall, but with that super-snob cachet of British exclusivity, you had to ring the bell to enter. Did I want to do that? No. Did I want to enter? I rang the bell.

A severe woman opened the door. Her straight dress was black, her stockings were black, her shoes, hair and eyelashes were black. So were her eyes, come to think of it.

Somewhere, perhaps under a damp dishrag, she had found the semblance of a smile, which she tried on briefly for me. She quickly decided it didn't suit her and she abandoned it. I didn't like it either. She looked like she had just stepped off a boat from one of those Muslim countries (the first-class deck) and found herself inadvertently in a distasteful commerce.

"Yes?" she said in that hollow-whiskey-gut-booming sound. She didn't move from the doorway.

"May I come in?" I asked in my best American hayseed tourist.

"I'm sorry, the gallery is closed."

I looked at my watch. "Oh," I said. It was a little after eleven. "What time do you open?"

"We will be closed until further notice," she said.

So why, I wondered, was she in the place, dressed like a matron in the washroom at Fortnum and Mason, if the joint was closed?

"I am an American here to look at and buy Impressionist art," I said. "I was told I should not miss Jacques Moran's. Couldn't I just take a quick run through?"

"I'm sorry, sir," she said as she backed away from the door and started closing it.

"Wait!" I exclaimed. "Let me talk to Mr. Moran. I have a letter of introduction to him."

She shook her head as severely as she was dressed. "Mr. Moran is not here."

"When will he be back?"

But the door was closed in my face.

A few doors down there was another art gallery. I stepped inside to be greeted by a young woman in a gray skirt and demure white blouse and a smile that didn't come from a can of Spam.

"Hello," she chirped in the voice of a songbird.

"Hello," I answered heartily. "What a pleasure to get a human response at a Bond Street gallery," I said.

"Oh. You haven't been well treated?"

"I just came from your neighbor." And I pointed down the street and shook my head with a puzzled look. I made like I was groping for the name of the establishment.

"Moran's," she supplied, but her accent was so clipped I wasn't sure at first what she was saying.

"Moran's. That's it."

"Oh, I'm sorry. I think Mr. Moran has disappeared, and no one knows what they're about, I'm sure."

"Do you know that dragon lady?"

She laughed. "You mean Madeline? I'm acquainted."

I shook my head. "Is she the boss?"

"I don't know exactly what her position is. I expect she was just doing what she was told. May I show you something?"

"Indeed. I'm into Impressionists."

"How nice."

"Mind if I look around?"

"Oh, please do," she said. "The Impressionists are in the room off to the right in the back. I wish we had more of them. It's my favorite period."

I sauntered through the gallery, one long room and several anterooms. In, as they say, "the States," if you go into an art gallery, the salesperson gloms onto you right away with a cheery "Hello," followed at varying intervals by "Are you a collector? Are you a visitor in town?" or what have you, in an effort to get the ball rolling, as though the gift of gab could sell art.

Maybe it does, but not to me. I try to communicate, without actually explaining, that the fine arts are a visual medium, not verbal. Though I'm sure they have *beaucoup* studies to show the blather sells.

This fine-looking woman was friendly and pleasant, but not pushy. I would have been nuts about her if I had just been perusing some gallery. Here, under my new investigative circumstances, I would have welcomed more interference.

The room off to the right in back was the size of a modest living room. It was hung with about two dozen works. One wall had drawings, another two, lithographs and etchings, and the final wall was devoted to paintings. A Monet, a Manet, a Degas, a Vlaminck, and I was happy to see our own Childe Hassam represented with one of his super flag works. Similar in some ways to the Monet flag painting that was the object of my search. There was also a small Renoir oil and zip Van Gogh. The auction houses had put that little painter, who during his lifetime was not able to sell a single painting, through the roof. Now we have books, movies, television about him. Life is a funny thing, especially when viewed after death.

Looking at these Impressionist paintings, I could see why they were so popular. Colors at once bright, cheery and muted, running into each other as though you were viewing some scene with half-closed eyes and seeing it in a way you never had before, yet in a way that somehow improved it.

It was the art of suggestion rather than its forerunner, representation. The invention of the camera had done a lot to make representative painting obsolete. Perhaps that was one reason the Impressionist works were commanding so much higher prices.

With time, the art of suggestion went so far that you were presented with a few blobs of color—or maybe only one blob in contemporary work. A black canvas might be a schoolground at night. To me it was just a black canvas.

But with Impressionism—you were looking at something differently, but you knew what you were looking at.

When I returned to the main room, the pretty woman stood at her desk. She was a nice five-and-a-half-feet tall, with that flawless skin you can only develop in the London fog. Michelangelo could not have done better with her features, and I suddenly wished I was fifteen years younger and footloose and phobia-free.

"May I answer any questions?" she asked cheerily.

"May I take you to lunch?" I blurted without thinking.

She looked more shocked than surprised. She frowned as though something was conspiring against the thought. When she spoke, it was as if from some dreamy séance: "I'd like that very much."

6

Her name was Sarah, and I was crazy about the name Sarah. It had a patina of old money to it, but I think if Sarah's name had been Dorcas I'd find something to love about it. She wore her hair like Joan of Arc and I couldn't get those shimmering blond tresses out of my mind. Nor could I forget her down-to-earth smile and the engaging dimples that went with it. I know the tough-guy private eye wouldn't let some skirt turn his head, but on a scale of Jell-O to steel, I was somewhere around wet grits.

Sarah wasn't available for lunch until one o'clock, but I would have waited a couple weeks anyway. In the meantime, I checked out some other galleries she said were up on Impressionists.

The best I got out of this bunch of galleries was a little deeper understanding of Impressionist art. I had already decided Monet was my favorite, though I thought he had to be the hardest to forge, with Matisse being the easiest to fake.

My fourth stop gave me my first feeling for the case. A tall, lanky gentleman happily delivered himself of his opinion of Jacques Moran. With a wave of his hand he offered, "Nobody around here takes him very seriously. He's a bit of a gadfly, you see."

"I was told he was the man to see for the rare Impressionist work," I said. I was seated at this desk in the cubicle in the back of his gallery that served as his office.

Little more than a small storeroom, the contrast to d'Lacy's digs amused me.

"Oh, he'll occasionally get his hands on a good-enough piece. But usually it's just dross."

"Were you aware he was peddling a Monet for ten million pounds or so? The flag picture?" I showed him a photograph.

"Heard some talk," he said, squinting at the photograph.

"Can you tell if that's a genuine Monet?" I asked.

"From this photograph, it looks like a rather poor forgery."

"How about this?" I handed him a second picture. He looked at it, then at the other, then back.

"Looks like the same picture taken in different light. Maybe different exposure or lens settings."

"You can't tell any difference?"

"I can't. Not from these photos."

"If I came to you for a picture like that, where would you look?"

"It's not a question of looking, in this business, for a masterpiece. Oh, we know where some are, but most of them stay put. It's not like real estate, where you send the owners letters asking if they want to sell."

"So you wait for people to come to you?"

"Not entirely. We have our sources who may be in a position to intercept someone bent on going to auction. But that's not easy—to get an owner to sell outright or on consignment after he's heard all the wonderful prices quoted by the auction houses. A lot of those prices are fake, you know."

"Do the sellers know?"

"Some," he said. "Some do, sure, but a surprising number of large-piece owners are naive about the auction houses."

"Well, I'd be interested to find this painting."

"What would you pay?"

"I think I have a client who would pay handsomely."

"d'Lacy?"

"Perhaps an insurance company."

"It's been stolen?"

"It's a possibility."

He looked at the pictures again and frowned. "Sometimes it's hard to tell from photos," he said.

My heart started to jangle as I approached Sarah's gallery. When I saw her through the window, standing, talking to a customer, I had to gasp a little air. She was so young and vibrant. So alive with all that was good in life.

The man was leaving as I walked in the door. "Live one?" I said to Sarah after he was gone.

She wrinkled her nose. "Rigor mortis."

We had a comfortable chuckle. A colleague of Sarah's came out from the back dressed very much like Sarah, but not half so beautiful. She looked at me, winked, and said, "Looks very much like the Yanks are coming."

Lot of good humor in this place, I thought, and Sarah and I wended our way through the crowded London streets to Fortnum and Mason for a greatly overpriced lunch.

I loved to see the men in tails prowling the floor of Fortnum and Mason, like a castle full of butlers who are anxious to be of service, perhaps ring up a jar of jam for you, or direct you to the men's.

Sarah had made the reservation. I think she had connections, because we were seated in the mezzanine area, where we could watch the floor.

I had trouble concentrating on the sparse menu the waitress handed me. I couldn't take my eyes off Sarah. She blushed.

"Forgive me," I said. "You're so beautiful."

Now we both blushed.

"Why, Mr. Yates," she smiled, "I'll bet you tell all the girls that."

"Believe it or not, I've never said that before."

"Well, it's a nice thing to say, in any case."

We ordered lunch. I thought to myself this was the kind of place they would cut the crusts off the bread, and they did.

"So what brings you to London, Mr. Yates?"

"I'll bet you ask all your customers that."

"Actually, no," she said with a twinkle in her eye. "Just the visitors."

We both had a good laugh.

"I came to see Jacques Moran. I had a letter of introduction. It was about a Monet. Then that dragon lady closed the door on me."

"That's Madeline," she said, shaking her head.

"What do you know about her and Moran?"

"Jacques Moran was a peripheral player in the art world. Made a living—nothing flashy. Then Madeline came along. Ever since, he's been like a lap dog to her. To all the world it looks like she's a cold fish, but she must do something, because he is a new man. He is traveling in wealthier circles, seems to have the inside track on a lot of big stuff. And all this happened since she came to work for him."

"How did they meet?"

She shook her head. "Don't know."

"The woman—Madeline—says Jacques is not here. He's gone. You have any idea where he could be?"

She shook her head again. "Word he took frequent trips to Switzerland. Came back with some up-market treasures."

"You ever see any of them?"

"No. They weren't put in his shop window. They went to special customers."

"Know any of them?"

"I don't, but I think Philip might."

"Philip?"

"My boss. Shall I ask him?"

"That would be—what is it you say? ducky."

"Ducky?" she laughed. "Some people say that, I suppose."

I took out my snapshots of the Monet. "You ever seen this painting?"

"No," she said, then looked closer.

"Does it look genuine to you?"

She peered at it for some time. "Do you have the original?"

"Yes."

"Can you take me to see it?"

"I'd love to. It's in Los Angeles."

She laughed again. It was so warming being in the company of a woman who laughed so infectiously.

"Funny," she said, looking at the pictures again, "I don't know this painting."

"Does anyone know them all?"

"Probably not. But Monet was my thesis—was going to be, before I decided I'd had enough school and it was time to sink or swim. I'm pretty familiar with Monet's work—I just can't place this. But I'll look it up."

"Aren't paintings sometimes discovered that no one knew the artist had painted?"

"Sometimes. The closer the artist lived to our time, the more unusual that is. We aren't sure Rembrandt did Rembrandt's. A lot of his students could do his signature paintings. But Monet is a different story. He was tracked every step of the way."

"But isn't it possible he did something that he showed no one? Something that got lost in the shuffle?" I asked.

"Possible?" She wrinkled her nose. "What *isn't* possible? I just don't think it's very likely. But I'll look it up. I could be wrong."

There was a bustle of movement on the store floor and in the restaurant at Fortnum and Mason, but it was as though we were on our own cloud, high above it all.

"Do you know the provenance of this work?" She

waved the picture at me.

"It's a little vague as I understand it. I'll try to do better."

"It could help."

"Do you have a fax machine at the gallery?" I asked.

"Sure."

"If you'll give me the number, I'll try to have it faxed to you."

I showed her the other picture. "Does that look the same to you?"

She compared the snapshots. "Pretty much. If it's not the same painting, it's an excellent copy." She handed the pictures back to me.

"How did you get into this art business?"

"The usual way," she said. "I went to art school. Got a degree in fine arts, painted up a storm. Got out, answered an ad, got the position. Thought I would do it to supplement my true work."

"Do you have any paintings I could see?"

"Why, Mr. Yates," she said. "Isn't that etchings?"

"Etchings? You did etchings?"

"Doesn't that cliché go, 'Come up and see my etchings'?"

"Oh, m—I'm sorry," I was stuttering. "I didn't mean..."

"Yes," she said, taking pity on my discomfort, "I have quite a stack of work I did some years ago, and I'd be flattered if you wanted to see them."

"Do you still paint?" I asked.

Her nose twitched. "When I have time."

"Why don't you take the time?"

"Well, you have to have the energy too. Selling is a rum go. On your feet all day long trying to cozy up to perfect strangers. It's a jolly tiring way to make a living."

"So why not give it up?"

"Because I do need to make a living," she said. "My life is salesmanship. I earn my modest living trying to sell other people's paintings. I can't sell my own. Rum go."

"I understand this forger—what's his name? The really good one...?"

"Oh, Albert Durant," she said.

"Yeah. I understand he can't sell any of his original artworks either, but he can make millions with forgeries."

"Yes, isn't that disgusting?"

"Have you seen any of his originals?"

"As a matter of fact, I have," she said.

"How are they?"

"Not bad, actually. He is a very talented man."

"Talented, but not original?"

"Maybe it's the fickle market," she said, finishing a crustless sandwich made and presented with loving British reticence. "He can make millions by convincing someone that a dead artist painted a picture. Why shouldn't the same painting command a similar price in the marketplace? It surely isn't his fault."

"Are you talking heresy?"

"Oh, probably. But it does go to prove, doesn't it, that the name is worth more than the work itself? A pity the Impressionists didn't know that when they were alive; they could have painted their names on paper bags and made a fortune."

"For their heirs, you mean. Not too many of them did too well while they were alive."

We passed up the dessert and I won the honor of paying the check; I having in this situation some need to impersonate a rich American. I walked her back to her shop. She suggested I talk to Rafer McKenzie, at the Royal Academy of Arts, for his take on Jacques Moran, and on my pictures.

I made a date with Sarah to see her paintings and take her to dinner. She returned to her vocation and I made my way across the street to the Royal Academy of Arts. There I was granted a few minutes with the curator of Impressionist work. He was a Scotsman who moved with a quicker grace than most of his countrymen. Fluid, of course, and gentle. But urgent. We stood at a counter in the reception area for the offices of the bigger wigs. Mr. McKenzie did not invite me into his office. Perhaps because I hadn't the grace to ask for an appointment.

He stood ramrod straight for our meeting, while I more or less leaned on the counter.

"Moran," Rafer McKenzie said, as though he were identifying a brand of cheese. "What can I tell you about him? Gone, is he? Perhaps he'll be back."

"I was given a letter of introduction to him by a museum director in the States."

"Which one?"

"Los Angeles."

"Oh, Franklin," he said, a slightly amused smile on his thin lips. "Franklin d'Lacy."

"You know him?"

"Everyone knows Franklin," he said. "If only by reputation."

Was I imagining it, or was he sneering? "And that's not good? His reputation, I mean?"

He pursed his lips in thought. "Bit of an ego, that one," he said. "Hard to bolster a reputation in this line if you let your ego show."

"Do you get the impression he is competent, knowledgeable—you know—knows his stuff?"

"Oh, I suppose he'll do for Los Angeles. Don't they call it Tinseltown? I can't think of tinsel without thinking of old d'Lacy. Seems to me he was made for Hollywood—or vice versa. Does he know his stuff? Depends what stuff you're referring to. Salesmanship? Superior. Self-promotion? None better. Fund raising? Near the top. Public relations? Good enough for his purposes. Getting people into the museum with glitzy shows? He wrote the book."

"Does he know art?" I asked.

"*Know* art," he said with disdain. "How can anyone *know* art? I don't think he's terribly educated at it—though he has impeccable taste."

"Do you think he could be fooled with a forgery?"

"My dear fellow, the dirty little secret of this close-knit fraternity is we can *all* be fooled by a master forger. I would hope that most of us could spot most forgeries in seconds. I've no reason to believe d'Lacy any more naive than the rest of us. Perhaps your question should be, is he good for the museum?"

"What would your answer be?"

"A man who isn't good for his museum—will not have his job long. Boards of directors are barracudas."

"What about Moran?"

"What about him?"

"You acquainted with his gallery?"

"Certainly."

"Have you bought paintings from him?"

"No."

"Would you?"

"Well, I suppose if the work was authentic and we could prove it, and the price was right."

"Has he ever tried to sell you anything?"

"Oh, there were a few things some years ago."

"But you never bought?"

"No."

"Why not?"

"A number of things. Shady provenance, suspicious of illegality—uncertainty about the legitimacy of the work—price too high for our budget, or more than I thought the piece warranted."

"Franklin d'Lacy has characterized him to me as a man of impeccable integrity with enviable standing in the art community—and a reputation as a connoisseur of Impressionist masters."

"He does, does he?" McKenzie frowned.

"Yes. What would you say to that?"

"I'd say it sounded like d'Lacy's usual Hollywood hype."

"You don't agree?"

"d'Lacy's hype is usually a little strong for me."

He had to run, he said. Though he was ever so charmed to meet me and would love nothing better than to talk to me forever, he had a board of directors to dance to, "and you know what barracudas they can be."

7

Since there was no telephone in my room in the inimitable Prince of Wales Hotel, I called Franklin d'Lacy from one of those delightful red phone booths on Piccadilly, across from the Royal Academy of Arts.

It was four-thirty in London—eight-thirty in the morning in Los Angeles. Franklin d'Lacy had told me he started his day at seven, so I could reach him. No one could call him a shirker.

In Europe, the phones, I discovered, are a little slower than in the States. After I placed the call, the operator promised to "ring you back."

It didn't take that long, but when you are used to an almost instant connection, it seemed like forever.

But finally he came on the line. He was hale and heartfelt. "Yates, good to hear from you. Everything going well, I trust?"

"For my first day I can't complain," I said.

"Good, good."

"Jacques Moran does not seem to be communicado," I said. "Would you have any idea where to look?"

"That son of a bitch better not have vanished with my painting. I told you he hasn't returned my calls."

"Do you know this woman, Madeline, who works for him?"

"Met so many, Yates, I don't know. What does she look like?"

I described her. "Yeah," he said, "the dark one—I met her. Cold fish."

"Think you could get her to talk to me?"

"Not if you can't."

"Well, if you think of any way to open her up," I said. "Now the painting, I think I'll need the provenance of the work..."

"What do you want that for?" He seemed to have a little edge in his voice.

I trod carefully. When things get tough blame others, is one of my many mottoes. "Everybody here says if I want to find this painting, I'm going to need the provenance."

"Who's everybody?"

"The art experts I've interviewed."

"Where?"

"Galleries—museums."

"Well, they don't know what they are talking about. Provenance is history, past, kaput. I can assure you none of the former owners will have the work."

He was definitely defensive. How to cut through it? Broadside. "Is there some reason you don't want me to have the provenance?"

"No, of course not!" he snapped.

"I have a pencil. It's not very long, is it?"

"No. But I don't have it right here. I'll have to get it and call you."

"Could you just fax it? I've got a number here. Be a lot better to have it written out."

There was a silence. I guess I wasn't acting like the powerful art mogul wanted me to. "What's the number?" he said, impatiently, as though I were detaining him by not volunteering the number. I gave it to him and asked him, kindly, to repeat it. He did. So much for the excuse of having written down the wrong number. But that still left "lost it" and all its variations.

"If I don't catch Moran going in or out of his gallery, do you have any idea where to look?"

"No. Maybe that dark woman."

"She doesn't seem inclined toward communication," I said. "Did you ever see him anywhere besides his gallery?"

"Had a few meals in restaurants."

"Which?"

"The Connaught... Then there's that coffee-shop chain on Piccadilly, near that bookstore—Hatchard's, I believe."

"Hatchard's is the bookshop, I think, not the restaurant."

"Right. We had a passable meal here and there, but the Connaught's the only place with real food."

"Did you stay there?"

"Yes, I did. Where are you staying?"

"Oh, you know, Mr. Hadaad can tell you I never divulge my residences. In this business—too risky."

"Suit yourself."

"Do you know anybody here who knows Moran?"

"Everybody knows Jacques Moran."

"But anyone in particular who might know where he is?"

"Sorry—not offhand."

"Well, if anyone comes to mind, add it to the fax, please."

"Where is this fax going?"

"An art gallery."

"*An art gallery*!?" he shouted. "Are you crazy? You're spilling the beans *there*? The grapevine in this business is ten minutes, worldwide."

"You have nothing to fear," I said. "Such details as I give do not involve you or your museum."

"So now I'm going on fax record?" he grumbled. "No, thanks. I'll fax your hotel."

"I'm afraid that won't be possible."

"Why not?"

"Two reasons—my residence remains my own business, and they don't have a fax machine anyway."

"I don't believe it. What kind of fleabag are you staying at that doesn't have a fax?"

"You put your finger on it, Mr. d'Lacy," I said. "Just remember, I don't get expenses."

"Yeah," he muttered.

"How about Albert Durant?"

"What about him?"

"I take it you know him?"

"I know *of* him. I never met him personally."

"What can you tell me about him?"

"Best forger in the business," he said. "A genius, really."

"Could he have painted your forgery?"

"No," he said, short on patience. "I already told you, this is art-student work. Durant would be insulted."

"I'm sorry," I said.

"No need to be. *I'm* not insulted."

"Do you think Durant could have painted the first painting?"

"No way."

"Why not?"

"Monet painted that."

"You're sure?"

"Sure as I've ever been."

"You realize no one I showed your pictures to can tell them apart."

"Is that so?"

"Either there is no difference, or you gave me half Monets or half forgeries."

"I'll check it out," he said. "Maybe I'm getting senile."

"Where would you look for Durant?"

"No idea. Where would you go if you were on the lam from the police?"

"Switzerland?"

"So look there," he said, hot under the collar buttons again. "But if you care at all what I think, find Moran. What will you get from Durant?"

"Well, if he forged the second painting, don't you think he would have had the first to work from? Maybe he knows where it went."

"I told you, there is no possible way Durant did that job. It's a botch."

"Maybe he did it under instructions. You know, 'Make a bad forgery.'"

"Why would he?"

"For money?"

"But what's the motive of his patron?"

"Embarrass you?" I asked.

There was a silence on the other end. "Possible," he muttered, "but you think if all that were true, he'd tell you?"

He had a good point, and I told him so.

"By the way," I said, "do you have any idea who shipped the painting?"

"Of course I do. Westminster Cartage, in the City of London," he said. "But I've already called them. Talked to all the drivers—everything. Nobody knows anything. Their reputation is unassailable."

"While I'm here, a personal visit wouldn't hurt."

"Suit yourself," he said unsuitably, "I think you're wasting your time." I was beginning to feel Franklin d'Lacy was going to be a hard man to please. Everything I suggested he pooh-poohed.

"Find Moran," he reiterated, "the rest of it is dead-end stuff."

"I'm looking for Moran. But sometimes the little insignificant things lead on to fortune. You don't get results in this game by leaving rocks unturned."

"Stones."

"As you wish." I reminded him to fax the stuff as soon as probable and he grumbled and hung up.

Sarah opened the door to my knock, and knocked the wind out of me. She wore a filmy multicolored skirt, rather long, that looked like it might have been painted by Gauguin. A yellow gauzy top complemented it.

"Can you come in a minute?" she asked. "I have something I'd like to show you."

Inside her modest flat, the walls were hung with Impressionist reproductions—mostly photographic, but a few lithographs, including Renoir's black study of Richard Wagner, and a Redon head of Christ with a crown of thorns—also black on white paper.

"Cheaper than color," she explained, when I noted she seemed to favor black-and-white original prints.

But the miracle of the place was the floor. It was covered with books.

"I didn't know you lived in a library," I said.

Sarah smiled. "I was quite an academic in a former mutation," she said. "I've been racking my brain over your pictures of the alleged Monet. After I left you I almost went nuts, and I didn't know why. Now I do. Here." She picked two books off the floor and the larger fell down again.

"Those books are too big to hold," I said. "I'll come to the books." I dropped to the floor and she came down with a liquid motion, as though she were crème fraîche.

"Look at this," she said, pointing to the two-page spread of a Monet painting called *Rue Montorgueil*, painted in 1878. It had lots of colored flags, all red, white and blue (for France), on multistory buildings. The Monet in question was similar, but while this scene seemed to be in spring or summer, our painting was a winter scene.

"Now look at this," Sarah said, showing me a picture of *View of London at Night*. The book said it was painted by Monet after 1900. He was teetering toward the abstract, Sarah said. "Look at the spots of bright color on the dreary background of dark buildings and dark sky."

"Yes," I said. I saw what she was talking about, but I didn't know what she was getting at.

"Now look at this," she said, pulling another book

center stage. It was opened to a picture of a painting called *Afternoon on the Avenue, 1917*, also known as *Flags, Afternoon on the Avenue.*

Then it hit me. My Monet picture was a clever conglomeration of all three.

"Isn't that brilliant!" she exclaimed.

"Well, I see what you're saying," I said, finally. "But this last painting isn't Monet, is it?"

"Good for you. It's a Childe Hassam," she said. "But a lot of the same feeling, wouldn't you say?"

"Well, there's a winter feeling to this one, all right. But it has a lot more flags."

"So beautiful." She virtually swooned, hugging a book to her bosom.

"What do you mean?"

"The execution, the creation, the blending of techniques. The irony."

"What's the irony?" I asked.

"The forger is using Hassam to authenticate a Monet that doesn't exist. Hassam aped Monet all the time. It's a case of the ape, aping the ape, aping the ape."

That was beyond my sophistication, but I said nothing to advertise my ignorance. But I didn't fool Sarah, so she explained—so tactfully, as if talking to herself to put all the pieces in place, rather than educating a dummy.

"I'll bet anything this is an Albert Durant. He's the only forger I can imagine who would have the wit and wherewithal to bring this off," Sarah said. "He's the ape— he's always the ape, aping some master. Well, Hassam was aping Monet, now Durant has turned the tables. Durant is aping Monet aping Hassam—instead of Hassam aping Monet—or Durant aping Hassam aping Monet. That would have offered him no challenge. And Durant is a man who thrives on challenge. Oh," she cooed, rocking the book at her bosom as though it were a baby, "the whole thing is just too delicious for words."

I was frowning. I was not unused to having people outreason me. But this woman was leaving me in the sand.

"Where does this Durant hang out?"

"When he's not in jail, you mean?"

"Jail?"

"Of course. He's chronic. He cannot stop forging. It's a disease with him—just as though he were an alcoholic or an obsessive gambler. So he's always in hiding. And always plying his trade, which is superb, almost undetectable forgery. Delicious!"

"How would you go about looking for him?"

"I'd ask Jane."

"Jane?"

"My friend. She used to date him."

"Date? Are you using that in its old-fashioned sense, or its contemporary sense?"

"The carnal sense," she said, and I knew we would get along famously.

8

When I asked Sarah for the best place in town for dinner, she countered with, "If money is no object?" Since I said it wasn't (foolish boy), we were dining at the Connaught. That super hotel in Mayfair.

Entering the corner door of the Connaught, you might think you were headed for a fairly upscale pub. Inside, you are put more in mind of a comfortable but unpretentious men's club, one whose membership requirements do not include a blood relationship to the royal family.

You enter the dining room through a long and narrow serving pantry, as though serving food had been an afterthought.

Once you are in the red-brown paneled dining room, higher expectations take over and are realized. The food that England was said to be incapable of producing is spectacularly produced here. With luck, you will get a waiter who is fairly adroit at the English language.

Often, however, his comprehension extends only to the English pronunciations, and the American dialects leave him on the icy side.

Our waiter was, I believe, Portuguese. I let Sarah talk to him and it seemed to work.

For the first course we had that wonderful cart park at the table and the layers revolve as they put a dozen delectable concoctions on your plate.

"Fantastic!" I said, biting into the menagerie.

"It's my favorite place."

"Do you get to come here often?"

"Sure," she said. "Every five or ten years, like clock-work." We had a nice laugh and I felt warmed that I was able to bring her here.

"Did you ever think of staying here?" she asked.

"Not until now."

"Where are you staying?"

"A place called the Prince of Wales."

"A hotel?"

"More or less."

"I don't know it," she said.

"I'm relieved to hear that." And we had another round of chuckles.

I'm afraid I wasn't much company for Sarah while I was experiencing the delights of the cart. She didn't seem to mind. When I finished my mming and ahing and my plate was clear I apologized to her.

"Not to worry," she said, "one sensual experience at a time, I always say."

I loved to laugh with Sarah. It was such a *good* feeling.

Tonight, in this half-lit atmosphere, Sarah reminded me of a younger Emma Thompson. A person full of fun who didn't take herself too seriously. Attractive, but in a down-home sort of way—not a magazine cover girl. Those girls always reminded me of sticks. Thousands of dollars a day for standing around while somebody took your picture. Body statistics that a minuscule portion of the population possessed. And a constant, often painful, struggle to maintain those statistics to keep working.

I always thought if I were of the female type with those peculiar much-sought-after stats, I would rather hustle hamburgers than be in such a dehumanizing occupation.

But then I wondered, what was so humanizing about the spot I was in? The million bucks at the end of the rainbow? The rest was prostitution, pure and simpleminded.

As we were smiling at each other like a pair of giddy

adolescents, I appended the silence.

"Sarah," I said.

"Hm?"

"Are you one hundred percent convinced that painting could not be a Monet?"

"Hundred percent? An absolute certainty? Is there such a thing?"

"Okay, but you're thinking in the range of ninety-nine?"

"Hey," she laughed, "you're nailing me to the floor."

"Where your books are?"

"Right. And you are right, no one can be certain. But I had a good time finding those similarities. But maybe Monet did paint another flag picture we don't know about. Apparently someone with sixteen million American dollars thought he did. And that in itself is persuasive evidence."

I was rubbing the frowns out of my forehead. "One thing I can't understand," I said. "My principal keeps saying the picture he got is not the picture he bought. Says anyone could tell the difference. Even I could, he says, without apparent need to diminish my art-detection abilities. Yet no art expert I showed the two pictures to would say they noticed a difference between them."

"That true?"

"You didn't, did you?"

"Let me see them again. Do you have them with you?"

I took the pictures out of my navy-blue blazer pocket and handed them to her. I was starting to dress like Michael Hadaad. She peered at them, then shook her head. "Looks to me like a bunch of pictures of the same painting."

"And it looked to me like the painting he showed me," I said. "Six pictures, one painting. All the same."

Looking up from the pictures, I was astonished to see the dragon lady from Jacques Moran's gallery come into the room with a man. She was in her all-black witch's costume and he was a short, squat, balding gentleman in a milk-chocolate jacket and yellow-spotted tie and some sort of striped shirt.

With my eyes, I directed Sarah to look to her left.

"What do you make of him?" I asked Sarah.

"Not British," she said. "Perhaps American."

"My thoughts exactly. You folks don't dress like that."

"No."

"Ever seen him before?"

She shook her head. "It's not Moran," she said.

"Doesn't look much like the picture I have," I said. "I'm going to talk to them."

Sarah frowned. "I don't expect you'll have much luck."

"If she has any manners at all, she'll introduce me to him."

"Don't count on it."

I got up and made my way to their table, where the waiter had just left with the drink order.

"Hello," I said effusively, as though we were such buddies she would be as glad to see me as I was to see her.

But Madeline only frowned.

"Good to see you, Madeline," I said, and turned to the brown-coated gnome across the table from her. I put out my hand. "I'm Gil Yates," I said. He didn't rise, but stared at my hand as if assessing his chances of being bitten. "Your name was?" My hand was hanging there like a mallard duck in the moment after being shot, before its plunge to the earth.

The "gentleman" looked up at me. Rather than confusion in his eyes, he showed me disdain. Madeline wasn't the only dragon in the bunch. "Do I *know* you?" he asked with the same grace he would employ to swat a fly.

"Gil Yates," I repeated, as though that should do.

"I heard what you said, but I'm sorry, I can't place you." His intonation was unmistakably American. Probably Queens.

I turned to Madeline for help. "Madeline," I said

with a plea in my voice. "Have you heard from Mr. Moran?"

"Sir," she said, fixing me with a withering eye that let me know she resented calling me "sir," and was only doing it with the strongest sense of irony. "Please leave us alone, or I shall hail the management."

Hail the management, I thought. What a delightful turn of phrase.

"Look," I pleaded, "I have come from the United States—Western United States, eight time zones away—in search of Mr. Jacques Moran. Can't you enlighten me to his whereabouts?"

"No, sir, I cannot," she said through clenched teeth which I was happy to see were not so hot: crooked and yellow.

"Because you don't know, or because you are unauthorized or afraid to tell?"

"Because it is none of your business!"

"Madam," I said firmly, "Mr. Moran has been in a rather large business transaction with my client. Things have not developed as promised. I'm sure I could straighten it all out by talking to Mr. Moran myself. Where can I find him?"

She gave me one of those long-suffering looks. Her lips could have strangled a worm, and her eyes told me I was that worm. "Mr. Moran left the office some days ago and has not been heard from since. I don't know where he went or why. There is no reason he should clear his movements with me. I am merely an employee." She said this last as though it was a fact that broke her heart.

"Are you in charge in his absence?"

She laughed, a bitter laugh. "In charge? I wouldn't know where to begin. The shop is closed until I hear from him—until he gives me instruction. Jacques Moran Gallery is Jacques Moran, full stop. Now you will kindly leave us alone or I shall have you forcibly removed from my table."

I turned to her friend, and put out my hand again. "Gil Yates," I said, "you were?"

He ignored me. I turned again to the dragon lady— she was summoning the maître d' with her imperial hand.

"If you hear from Mr. Moran, please tell him an agent of Mr. d'Lacy is looking for him."

She pursed her lips and continued hailing the maître d'. I went back to the more congenial companionship of Sarah.

I was up with the sun the next morning. The trucking business was an early-bird enterprise.

Artie McMullin looked like an upscale neurosurgeon. He was the dispatcher for the London hauling firm of Westminster Cartage.

I met him on the loading dock, where he was yelling instructions across a wall of crates and over the drone of the diesel-truck engines. He had a clipboard in hand and now and again waved it to indicate a truck or driver or just a pile of goods.

He looked like a man who took neurosurgery seriously. When I introduced myself and told him what I was after, he smiled wanly, as if to say, "This I need like a hole in the head." But he took me into his disastrous office and removed a pile of lading documents from a straight metal chair and bade me sit down.

"Yates?" he said. "Is that as in Rowdy Yates, that Clint Eastwood character on the telly?"

"Why, yes, you know the program?"

"*Rawhide*? You bet. I never missed it—and I belong to the club that has it all on tape."

"It's a common name," I said. "Of course, we're not related."

"Yes," he said. "How could you be?—it *was* a fictional character, wasn't it?"

"Yes." I didn't tell him mine was fictitious as well. I could have introduced myself as Malvin Stark, but he was of the era where Jerry Lewis, that ersatz commedian, made so much fun of the name Malvin. I'll never forget him in that broader-than-all-outdoors screwed-up face of his smirking. "MALLL-*VIN*?" I wasn't unhappy to have bestowed upon my person a pseudonym.

With less fanfare than it took to say good morning to the Queen, we seated ourselves amid what looked like the aftermath of the London blitz.

"Excuse the mess, will you," he said. There was no question there. "Now, this painting business—I don't mean to cut it short, but I have gone over it with that Delancy chap from the States."

"d'Lacy," I corrected him, needlessly, "with a lower-case 'd' and an apostrophe."

"Yes, of course," he said, "he would have.... At any rate, we checked it every step of the way and while the shipment was in our hands nothing untoward occurred."

"What *could* have happened while you had it?" I asked. "I mean, could you trace the trip for me, along with how many people had access to the crate with the painting?"

He sighed the sigh of the put-upon, and opened a lower desk drawer and leafed through some folders, finally extracting one and, making a small clearing on his desk, spreading it out there.

"We picked the shipment up on Thursday morning the eleventh. About nine a.m.—apparently—from the Jacques Moran Galleries in New Bond Street. From there, it was taken directly to British Airways for shipment to Los Angeles on a direct flight." He spread his hands as if to say, "You see—foolproof."

"Did the driver know what he had?"

"Yes. He was picking up from an art gallery, after all, and the parcel was shaped like a painting."

"Did he know the value of it?"

"Yes."

"What can you tell me about the driver?"

"Tell you? He's worked for us thirty-two years. As honest as they come. No flummoxing there, I'd stake my life on it."

"Was that the usual way to ship a parcel of that value?"

He shrugged his shoulders, and his charcoal-gray cardigan sweater lifted, then seemed to stay up long after his shoulders went back down. "Often with cargo of that value, a messenger would escort it personally."

"You mean, fly with it in an adjoining seat?"

He nodded.

"Why didn't they...?"

"Don't know. Our record and reputation are impeccable. We did give it special treatment."

"How so?"

"We did it solo."

"Solo?"

"Yes, one pickup and delivery. There was nothing else on the lorry. He made no stops."

"They pay extra for that service?"

"Of course."

"Who paid?"

"It was prepaid. We wouldn't do it any other way."

"By Jacques Moran?"

"Yes."

"So what happens from there?"

"It is loaded on the plane."

"Right away?—or does it sit somewhere first?"

"We timed the delivery so it could be special handled—and loaded without sitting around."

"Would there be time anywhere to switch paintings in the crate?"

"Only before we picked it up," he said.

"What happens on the other end?"

"It is off-loaded and stored in customs warehouse."

"Can anyone get to it there?"

"Only in the movies," he said.

"So if the painting were switched, you say—"

"Most likely when it was crated."

"But d'Lacy watched the packing."

"He wasn't there when we picked it up. They could

have shipped a different crate entirely."

"Do you think that's what happened?"

"I have no idea if *anything* happened. I am speculating on a chain of events known to me. We are shippers. We don't open the crates. We don't have x-ray vision. It does seem strange, however..." he trailed off, looking out his window to the frenetic activity on the dock, which he longed to join. He stood up. "I'm sorry, I have to get back to earning my pay..."

"What does?" I asked.

"Pardon?" His mind was already gone from my subject.

"What seems strange to you?"

"Oh, that," he said, looking at the papers on his desk as though they, and not I, were the real intruders. "All this fuss," he said, "and I haven't seen an insurance claim. If I'd lost something worth sixteen million, I'd make a claim..."

We shook hands. I thanked him. He said, "Pleasure."

9

From Artie McMullin at Westminster Cartage, I stopped at London's answer to the International Pancake House for breakfast. It was a place that exhibited an irreverence for refrigeration, but everyone on the staff spoke pretty good English.

From there, I walked to Sarah's gallery where I waited a few minutes for it to open, before I decided to give Jacques Moran another try. I knocked at the door bracing myself for the ice maiden, but no one answered the door. I got back to Sarah's gallery as they were opening the door.

Inside, Sarah greeted me with her unforgettable smile, and handed me the fax from Franklin d'Lacy. It gave me a sketchy idea of the provenance of the Monet painting:

> *Monet gave the painting to a Giverny butcher, August Chaumount, in exchange for meat for an undetermined period. The butcher was no art lover but apparently hung the Monet in his home. When he died, c.1937, the picture fell into the hands of his adopted son, Andre Chaumount, who "couldn't make heads or tails of it." He found the painting*

ugly and buried it among his clutter in the attic of his home in the outskirts of London. At his death, in 1993, Phillipe Rogier, the apparent heir, was inventorying the contents of the Chaumount home when he came across a painting signed "Monet," whose work and sig nature he recognized as being of some value. He took it to the Jacques Moran Gallery for appraisal. The work was appraised at $18,500,000, and sold to Jacques Moran for $16,000,000 less gallery com-mission.

In Franklin d'Lacy's hand was appended to the bottom of the page, this note:

"As you know, the sixteen million was supplied to Jacques Moran by LAMMA and yours truly. The crating of the painting for air shipment was supervised by me personally. Somewhere, at some time between shipment and delivery, the painting was removed from its case and a forgery was put in its place."

I asked Sarah, "What do you make of it?"

"Not that unusual, I guess." She hummed a droning sound as she considered it again.

"Something wrong?" I asked.

"I don't know. Something seems a little peculiar, but I'm not sure what it is."

"You'll be sure to tell me when it comes to you?"

She nodded as though she was not listening. "Oh, look," she said, peering at the fax machine, "here's something else."

It was a note from d'Lacy:

"Found picture of Monet. Gave you several of the other "painting" by mistake. I'm checking into the Alzheimer's ward in the morning. If I remember. Will mail pix when you give me address."

Since it was one-thirty in the morning in Los Angeles I put off calling d'Lacy.

"Where would you turn now?" I asked Sarah. She wore another white blouse and gray skirt. It was like a gallery uniform. The two other women had the same ensemble on.

"Shall I see if I can get Jane to get you a meeting with Albert Durant?"

"The forger? Too good to be true. You think you could?"

"Try," she said. "No promises." She went through the rigmarole required to get a long-distance line in the gallery.

"Jane!" she said, turning the volume up to be heard across the English Channel. "How have you *been*?"

I could feel the excitement in the air.

"What's new, Jane—are you still seeing Albert?... Oh, dear... Yes, yes... I've just met a chap myself... Yes, isn't it?" Sarah rolled her eyes toward me. "Yes, he's a bit of all right..." She winked at me. "Anyway, I have a favor to ask of you... Yes... My chap—Gil Yates is his name.... Yes, isn't it?..." she laughed. I wasn't let in on this one. "He's trying to find a painting that was substituted with a forgery. He's got photos of the forgery—maybe Albert would know who might have painted it... Yes, I know he is... I know.... Yes, I know... Okay—will you ring me back?... Thanks, Jane."

She hung up and turned to me for my briefing. "Albert is apparently acting up again. He and Jane are on again, off again. Albert is a man of fiery passions, which can be fun sometimes, but a real pain the rest of the time.

Apparently he is on the warpath about something, so she's going to feel him out to see if there's any chance he'd talk to you without chewing your head off. She's going to ring me back."

"Shall I wait?" I asked. "I mean, can I do something in the meantime or...?"

"No, go on. It could take two days for Albert to answer his phone," she said. "What's on for today?"

"Lunch and dinner?"

"At least," she said.

"I'm going to try to hire someone to watch for Moran going in and out of the shop. You don't happen to know where he lives?"

"No, but I should know someone who does," she said, writing a note to herself at her desk out on the gallery floor.

When we met for lunch, Sarah had Moran's home address, a neighborhood of pleasant flats in Knightsbridge, she said. With the sixteen-million coup, I expected he might be moving up a bit. After lunch I taxied out there, and met, across the street from Moran's pad, every detective's dream, a kindly old busybody who rocked away her days and nights at her bay window.

"No, I haven't seen Mr. Moran for four or five days now," she said. "Perhaps he's on holiday."

"Perhaps," I agreed, and thanked her for her help.

Fortunately there was only a front door to the Moran Gallery, so I got away with hiring one dick to watch for Moran. The Westpark Agency made copies of my photographs and covered the door twenty-four hours. I was spending my money like it was going out a mile.

At four-thirty I called d'Lacy.

"Gil—glad you called—it's heating up here. You have anything that gives you any hope?"

"For a day and a half, I have a lot of hope. I am spending money like it was Pepsi-Cola, so I was getting a queasy feeling—what if I produce the goods, and the goods aren't the right goods?"

"What the hell do you mean?" d'Lacy seemed put out.

"Well, for starters, where is the million to come from?"

"What million?"

I was struck dumb. A lot of costly transatlantic phone time passed without being plagued with conversation. "My fee," I croaked.

"Oh, that—yes, your fee." Silence.

"So where will it come from? Your personal account?"

"The fee, yes," he answered vaguely. "Didn't I tell you if you got your hands on that painting, you'd have a six-teen-million-dollar asset? Anybody, and I mean anybody, would gladly give you a million for it. And if you took the million, you'd be the victim of the biggest screwing since the Indians unloaded Manhattan for twenty-four bucks' worth of beads."

"Sounds good," I said. "Except for one thing."

"What's that?"

"I don't have title to the painting."

"All right, you sell it to the insurance company. They save fifteen million. They ask no questions. You'll be a hero to them."

"So that's it. To get my fee I have to scam the insurance company?"

"I'll do it for you," he said, as though he had offered to go to the corner for a loaf of bread.

"So there does not now exist a legitimate account with the one million in it—in the event I deliver?"

"Well, no, why would there be?"

"Only for my sake," I admitted, "not for yours. I guess I was a little hasty trusting you, Mr. d'Lacy. Bowled down by your glittering celebrity, I guess."

"You have nothing to fear, believe me."

"No? I see myself spending twenty, thirty thousand, easy—schlepping all over Europe, paying other dicks to cover what I can't."

"You said guys who asked expenses were small-timers. You big-timers get big fees. Phone calls and hotel rooms are small potatoes."

"Granted," I said. "If I get the fee."

"Don't be so paranoid."

"Thanks for the advice," I said. "Here's what I will need to continue jackassing all over the world for you."

"Hey, wait a minute," d'Lacy said. "You took the job. You didn't ask for advances, you knew the terms—now all of a sudden you got cold feet. How come?"

"Icy cold feet," I agreed. "How come? I'll tell you. There's a lot of weird stuff here. So I can handle that. What I can't handle, or understand, is how I am going to get a legitimate fee out of this."

"I just told you," he said with that impatience in his voice he was so adroit at using on those he felt inferior, "the insurance company…"

"Sorry, I'm not scamming for my fee. I get paid, just like a doctor, a lawyer or a museum director."

"Jesus, Gil, don't hold me up like this now," he pleaded. "All hell is breaking loose here and my neck is in the noose."

"Exactly!" I said. "And where does that leave me and my thirty-grand investment after they hang you out to fry?"

"Say, Gil, Jesus, can't you ever get one of those clichés right?"

"A million bucks in a Swiss account," I said, talking tough. Sometimes talking tough could make you feel tough. I'm not sure if it ever worked with me. It didn't now. "Two signatures to get it out. Mine is one of them."

"Oh, my God, Gil—there isn't going to be a mil without the Monet. Not even a hundred thou."

"Well—you decide. Talk to Hadaad. He might stand you the sum."

"Michael's been a brick. I can't ask him that," he said. "Don't you see what's happening to me? They're trying to screw me out of my job with this forgery. They don't believe it was switched."

"Who doesn't?"

"The birds on the board of the museum. The guys whose tune I dance to. The ones who would rather have another dancer."

"A majority?"

"Damn near. One or two more get cold feet, I'm a cooked goose. Can you actually believe that anyone with the slightest sense would think a man of my experience could buy that piece of cheese for sixteen million and think it was a Monet?"

"So if I understand your position, I'm at even more risk," I said into the telephone. "All the more reason I need some better guarantee."

"You are a hundred-and-ten-percent guaranteed. You bring the Monet, you'll get your money. I'm giving you my personal guarantee."

"Well, think it over," I said. "I'm amenable to any screenplay that provides the million in advance—instantly available."

"Believe me, Gil, you have the painting, you'll have the money. If we don't pay—you keep the Monet."

"How long till the coppers come down? I'm going to hold a hot painting for ransom? Come on! If you think I'm that dumb, you made a terrible mistake hiring me."

"I'll see what I can do," he said wearily. "In the meantime, do you want this picture?"

"Sure, send it the quickest way short of a messenger in a plane—to my attention to the Peter Gallery." I gave him the address. "By the time it gets here I hope you'll have a solution. I have to go to Switzerland, and who knows where else. Time is the wine—isn't it?"

"The essence. Time is of the essence."

"I knew it had something to do with wine."

He bid me adios, and I reminded him to get the money where I could get my hands on it.

10

Sarah was getting more wrapped up in the case than I was. Her eyes sparkled and her skin throbbed when we discussed the dilemma of the missing Monet.

As we did that night at dinner. My plea for a firmer fee with d'Lacy notwithstanding, I offered to take Sarah back to the Connaught, but she wanted something simpler.

"Gosh, Gil, we can't eat like that every night. I'd blow up like a balloon and your bank account would just blow up."

That night, cozy in her flat, Sarah Collins said, "How long can you stay in London?"

"Not long enough," I said.

"Want to save some money?"

"Always."

"You could stay here."

"What a nice offer," I said. "You really are a generous spirit."

"Does that mean selfish? That might be more accurate."

"No—I was just thinking, I really like it here. Why should I care if someone switched a painting or not?"

"We'll have a better idea when we get the picture of the original. If there was an original."

"And if we get the picture."

"I just thought of something—with all this *if* talk. Did you ever see the canceled check for sixteen million?"

"No."

"Shouldn't you?"

"Good idea," I said, then I considered it. "Trouble is, Franklin d'Lacy's getting a shorter fuse. All he wants is his picture, and he doesn't have a lot of patience when I seem to be investigating him, as I would be, asking for that check."

"But you could be interested in the information on the back. Where it was deposited, by whom? When? It might help you find Moran—et cetera."

"I'll call when I get the photograph of the Monet painting, I might have some questions. Besides, I want to give him a some time to find a way to lock in my fee."

"You know what?" Sarah said.

"What?"

"We're off the subject."

"The subject was...?"

"Staying here. I'd be happy to have you."

"Oh, thanks, but I think I've got to keep that gnat-bag as a headquarters. It wouldn't do if I didn't have a home base." Of course, I thought to myself, they don't know where I'm staying. But with my wife having my address it was just as well...

"Oh, wow," she said, when I showed her the photo of the Monet two days later. "that's more like it."

Even I, as d'Lacy had predicted, could see the difference. Easily. And what a beautiful painting. Haunting was the word. It certainly looked like d'Lacy and LAMMA had been conned, big time.

"Look like a real Monet?" I asked her.

No hedging this time. "It does to me," she said.

I spent the morning showing the picture around the art shops of London, asking if anyone had seen the painting. No one had, but admiration for it was virtually unanimous, and no one said it was over-priced at sixteen million American dollars. (A little under eleven million British pounds at the time.)

At lunch, Sarah told me her friend Jane had called. Albert Durant had grudgingly consented to see me, but she said he is so erratic lately that I could be rebuffed for days. If I wanted to come to Zurich, I would have to be prepared to sit it out until the spirit moved him.

After lunch I got my plane ticket for Zurich. Sarah wanted to go along but realized she also needed a job.

I checked with the Westpark agents. No Moran coming or going. I asked them to take Polaroid pictures of anyone who went in or came out of the Moran gallery, and to give them to Sarah to overnight to me in Switzerland.

I knocked on the closed door of the Jacques Moran Gallery again.

The dragon lady appeared. "You!" she said. The view didn't make her happy. She started to shut the door.

"Wait a minute," I said, holding out the picture. "You ever seen this?"

Her eyes flashed. "Where did you get that?" She started to grab for the picture. I withdrew it. "Oh, no," I said. "Hear from Mr. Moran yet?"

"No," she barked. "And I do not know where he is or when he'll be back. Now where did you get that picture?"

"Recognize it?" I taunted her.

"I certainly do."

"Know where it is?"

"We shipped it to Los Angeles—the museum."

I shook my head. "Didn't get there."

She opened her mouth to speak, when the short, bald guy I saw at the Connaught in her company came to the door and pulled her back. "Why are you talking to that man?" he said, and closed the door in my face.

Sarah said she wanted to take me to the airport, but since she didn't have a car, I made my way to Heathrow on the underground and bus.

I checked my bag and had time for a couple calls.

First to d'Lacy.

"Oh, Gil," he said, sounding a bit down.

"Got the picture. What a difference."

"Well, you can see my problem. That's what I bought and packed; the other comic-book copy is what I got. It's so damn depressing, and such an insult that whoever pulled this didn't have the decency to have a good forgery made. Something that might have fooled somebody. The whole thing makes me look like a moron." There was a heavy sigh on his end. "The paper is starting in on me now."

"What are they saying?"

"You don't want to know. Gil?"

"Huh?"

"Just get me that painting, will you?"

"Love to. If I knew where it was."

"It has to be there somewhere. The European art market is fairly inbred and not that huge. Are you seeing any light in the tunnel?"

"Not much. Still no Moran. I'm having his shop watched twenty-four hours. Hasn't been home in six or seven days now. Hasn't been seen at the gallery. Oh, by the way, the dragon lady seemed quite put out that I had the picture of the Monet."

"I wonder why?"

"She was in on it?"

"I don't know what you mean. She seems to be Moran's assistant, so I'm sure she was aware if not really part of the scam."

"You think the Moran Gallery made the switch?" I asked.

"I'm beginning to wonder."

"You don't think it could have happened on your side of the Atlantic? The switch, I mean?"

"Much harder once the box is in customs here. The Europeans have more connections with people who are willing to pay for stolen art. I'm starting to wonder about Moran—where has he gone and why? Flight is evidence of guilt in this country. I suggest you concentrate on finding him. He's got to have some answers."

"Any progress on my fee?"

"Oh, Gil, Jesus, you don't know what I've been through here. I'll tell you, I've been through such hell, I'm beginning to wonder if I couldn't have been set up by my own board. Voting me out wouldn't do it for them. I'm too damn popular with the public. No, they've got to humiliate me in the bargain. It's just so damn astonishing the things the public will swallow."

"So you've no solution to put my mind at ease about my fee?"

"Jesus, Gil, I'm working on it, between dodging reporters and fending off unfriendly calls from directors—believe me, you have nothing to worry about," he said.

But I wasn't sure I believed him. But one thing I couldn't help feeling better about—the painting by Monet. It was a real stunner.

It was my third full day in London and I had barely thought about my wife. I didn't think about my job, but three days was an unusually long separation for me from my palms. I decided to call Tyranny Rex to check on my palms.

I had another half-hour to flight time so I put in a call to the Tyranny. "Well, it's about time I heard from you," Tyranny said after the connection was made.

"Oh, did you have something to tell me?" If size and formidableness were the only criteria, she could do a Brunhilde.

"No."

"Did I get some great mail?"

"No."

"How's the weather?"

"All right."

"Hot?"

"Not particularly."

"Windy?"

"No," she sighed. "You're just asking me these questions because all you care about are your damn palm trees. Well, no, I didn't check on them, and, yes, they all seem to be still standing. Of course, there are so damn many of them there isn't room for any of them to fall over."

"Thanks," I said. I always used a soft tone with Tyranny Rex. Not that I expect it to get me any farther. Not that it did. I guess I just thought raising my voice would only aggravate her. Someday I intend to put that theory to the test.

Not today. "Say, Dorcas, you didn't happen to look at the paper today...?"

"I did *so*," she answered, as though challenged.

"You didn't happen to see anything about any art business at the L.A. Metropolitan, did you...?"

"Well, I did *too*."

"Really? What was it?"

"I don't know," she said, "something about some French painting they suspect isn't authentic or something. Looks like that loudmouthed director could be in the soup this time."

"Oh? Who's a loudmouth?"

"Oh, that museum guy. He's always in the papers, going on about something."

"So what are they doing about it?"

"Nothing I can see. It was just one of those short pieces that stirs people up without telling them anything," she said. "Say, since when are you interested in art?"

"Oh, I'm not really. I just heard some scuttlebreast here while I was browsing in a gallery to get out of the rain. Curious, is all. In L.A. we have one of the few art celebrities in the world. Franklin d'Lacy seems to be known here in London."

"You might be too if you were always shooting off your mouth the way he is."

"What's he saying?"

"They pulled a switch on him. He bought the real goods. They sent a fake."

"Hm, could happen, I suppose," I said. "Everything all right there?"

"Well as can be expected."

"Daddy Wemple making out all right?"

"I expect so. Haven't seen him, really."

"Could you check my palms today or tomorrow? I put some smaller ones in and I'd like to make sure Amanda is watering them enough." Amanda was the girl down the street who I paid to water the palms in my absence. Tyranny would have nothing to do with it.

"That's Amanda's job," she said. "She knows better than I."

"Well, will you just *look* at them sometime?"

She grumped and said she would.

"I'll call again," I said. It was news that didn't seem to thrill her.

I stepped away from the phone and heard my flight called.

A gentle rain was falling. It would lubricate the sky for my flight to Zurich and the legendary Albert Durant.

Then I began to wonder, wasn't it even *more* dangerous to fly in the rain? Visibility was down, runways were slick, and didn't all that water affect aerodynamics adversely?

11

I was shocked to see this statuesque blond smiling broadly at me after I cleared customs.

"You must be Gil," she said.

"How come?" I asked.

"I'm Jane." She put out her hand and I would have been a fool not to take it. "You Gil, me Jane," she said, with the most engaging smile.

Holy smokes, I thought. Another fantastic woman. My second thought was I was disappointed Sarah wasn't jealous of this gorgeous woman who could have buried all the supermodels under the curve of her palm. My third thought was some higher power was compensating me for my life sentence to Tyranny Rex by throwing all these gorgeous, super young women at me. The last thought I remember was how ungracious it would be of me not to oblige them with my most serious attention.

"Come along," she said, "you're staying at my place."

"Your place?"

"Yes. I don't know how else you'll get to see Albert. He's so erratic, you've just got to be around in case he shows up."

I couldn't think of a good argument—except Sarah, of course. That ridiculous song from *Finian's Rainbow* started running through my head:

When I'm not near the girl I love,
I love the girl I'm near.

Jane had one of those little foreign cars that ran like a sewing machine. We folded ourselves inside and were on our way.

On our ride from the airport to Jane's apartment, I noticed in Zurich a similar feeling to London. They are two human-sized cities—not like those megacities that compete for the most sun-blocking buildings.

You can walk down the streets here without feeling like a flea.

Jane's apartment was larger and fancier than Sarah's. Jane not only looked like a model, she was. Some of her layouts were lying around the place. She had a living room and a bedroom. Her windows in the front looked out on a grassy little park.

"Please be at home here," she said, and we sat on the couch while she told me what a difficult guy Albert Durant was.

"First of all, he's scared to death of the police. He realizes all he has to do is stop forging paintings and the police will gladly leave him alone. But he can't. It's a disease with him. He has this mad obsession with expressing himself through the masters. When he expresses himself through himself he doesn't make a penny. And that makes him even crazier. He's become a recluse."

"But how hard would it be for the police to find him?"

"Not hard at all. They know where he is, and he knows they know. It's just his phobia. On the one hand, he *is* committing fraud; on the other, I think the cops recognize his victims act out of the wrong motives and they are just as happy to see them duped. There is something lovable about a con," she said.

"Yes, you too? I've always thought that. Of course, if you were ever the victim, you might feel differently."

"I suppose. But how would we be victims of a swindle like this? Albert works in the millions. He's fooled some pretty big fish."

"Hm."

"I really think the only way the police would arrest Albert again was if he made a transaction at the police station, signed an affidavit it was a forgery, and spit on the police chief."

We laughed together. Laughing together was a nice feeling. I felt good with Jane. I felt good with Sarah. This, for a classic wimp from the States, was an embarrassment of riches.

I could hardly take my eyes off Jane. She stood about a half-inch taller than I did, wore the softest looking black sweater—cashmere, I speculated—and a skirt that had the look of black leather. She had braided her hair and wrapped the braids in a circle in back.

How did she compare to Sarah? Taller, more expensive clothes, sexier, bigger and better apartment, but also a little more showbiz. I decided Jane's thoughts never strayed far from herself. All the same, a repressed nerd like me could hardly help but be overwhelmed by her beauty and proximity.

"I've got an early call tomorrow," she said. "I've set you up for Albert at ten. Will that be all right?"

"Super."

"I expect he will call to cancel, but I suggest you don't answer the phone. Just show up. He'll complain bitterly, but I expect you'll get to talk to him."

"Show up where?"

"Oh, didn't I tell you? Sorry. His place. I'm surprised he agreed. Doesn't receive visitors often. I will leave you a map before I go in the morning. I leave at five—I don't expect you'll be up."

"Well, I..."

"Now all that's left are the sleeping arrangements," she said matter-of-factly. "I'd like you to take the bedroom—I'll do the couch."

"Oh, no," I insisted, "I'll be fine on the couch."

"No, no, I'm getting up early, you take the bedroom so I won't disturb you."

"I'm not putting you out of your room," I insisted. "You don't have to worry about disturbing me."

"No, really..." she said, then stopped to laugh. "You know how we could solve this the simplest way?"

"How?"

"We'll both take the bedroom."

I expect you're wondering about those "sleeping arrangements." I don't think, under the circumstances, it would be gentlemanly to disclose exactly what transpired. But a few points might be conceded: One, I am a man whose life has been one long bout with repressed sexuality. Two, my wife of a couple decades plus, is not a woman with a penchant for the sensual. Three, consequently, I hardly realized that women with these "appetites" existed. Four, a starving man when presented with the opportunity may very well gorge himself on sweets.

That's about all I'm willing to say about it, except that her sweater *was* cashmere and the skirt a very soft glove leather—both sides.

She didn't wake me when she left at five in the a.m.—I hadn't been to sleep.

I did sleep after she left, and was only awakened by the ringing of the telephone at nine sharp. I reached for the phone groggily, then came to my senses. Jane said Albert Durant would call to cancel and I shouldn't answer the phone—so I didn't. But luckily I was awakened—or I would have blithely slept through the appointment he was trying to break.

The map to Albert's was on the table. I had had a fantasy that Jane would have wanted me to stay with her longer and would have conveniently forgotten to leave the map. No such luck. Well, maybe Durant wouldn't be there—wouldn't answer the door, or would just refuse to talk to me. I could always hope.

On the way to Albert's digs, in a taxi, I reminisced about my plethora of good fortune, women-wise. I was still a little disappointed that Sarah seemed so willing to let me stay with Jane. Maybe she thought she was a lesbian or something.

The cab pulled up in front of an engaging villa. My first thought was, Jane was right. How could anyone hide in a spread like this? The cops didn't want him.

The old Tuscany house was set back on a small knoll and fairly well hidden behind assorted shrubbery and trees. I paid the driver enough to buy a cab company in Los Angeles. Luckily the tip was included in the fare or I would have been forced to file for bankruptcy. Or, as they say, do a Chapter 11 (in Chapter 11).

I realized, when he drove off toward the city, I could be stranded here without seeing the master forger at all. I would be, as they say, bussing it back to town.

The air was so clear here in Zurich and its environs. The sun made everything sparkle, just as the fog in London seemed to tarnish that city.

I walked up the irregular stone path. Irregular? Half the stones were missing and the other half were so askew you took your life in your hands making your way to the front door. Albert Durant was sending his message: Scram!

I felt in my pocket for the pictures. I looked at my watch and saw I was a couple minutes early. What to do? Durant was such an erratic cuss he just might blow up over five minutes. So I stood my ground on his front stoop–a flat-tish rock that couldn't seem to find its level—until that big hand got to the twelve.

Whereupon, I knocked.

Then I knocked again.

And again. I tried the door, gently turning the knob, as they do in these epics. It was locked.

There seemed to be a rustling in the bushes on the

far side of the house. I moved carefully in that direction, but saw nothing. Perhaps it had been an animal.

I looked in a window on the front side. The room was strewn with junk: boxes, bags, papers, magazines. It looked like the pad of a derelict.

I heard the noise again and went to the far side of the house—a veritable jungle on the hills overlooking Zurich. Only there wasn't any "overlooking" from this vantage point–the vegetation had taken over.

Again the sounds of rustling footsteps disturbed me and, not given to mindless heroics, I hid in the bushes and moved in this thicket toward the sounds. Of course, I was making shocking sounds of my own—and as soon as I could see beyond the back corner of the house, I saw the back of a man leaving the property in haste. His back was to me. From my glimpse of his clothing and his carriage, he did not seem like a poor man, nor like a burglar. He wore a dark-blue blazer and gray pants, had dark hair—I'd even say black—and he seemed to have a scar under his hairline, almost the width of his neck. Like he got too close to a guillotine.

He moved swiftly. I moved slowly. He got away. Thank goodness. I am not one for dramatic confrontations. I am, I confess, a bit of a coward. I can't imagine any situation that tested my strength that would see me come out of it anyway but badly battered.

I looked in the back window nearest me and found myself looking into a kitchen of incredible disarray. It looked like the last dish had been washed before the Second World War. In fact, the shape of the kitchen was enough to convince you that Switzerland's neutrality in that war was a fiction. They were heavily involved, and the major battles took place right in this kitchen. I knocked on the back door.

No answer.

I tried the door. Open. Dilemma: Do I walk through the house and stumble on a dead body as people usually do in the movies, or do I mind my own business and go back where I came from?

All logic and discretion was on the side of the latter.

But where I came from was so far away. Besides, maybe he wasn't dead.

I stepped inside. "Mr. Durant?" I called out. No answer. The place was still, like empty houses are. Some shifting of position and repeating the call, "Mr. Durant—Albert Durant?" produced no response.

As I went from room to room—kitchen, bathrooms, bedroom—I thought one thing was certain: This genius was a pig.

There, on the ground floor (there were two stories), I came upon his studio. It smelled of fresh oil paint. It was in disarray, but nothing like the rest of the house.

On the easel was a painting that might have been his own. It didn't look like a forgery of any work I had ever seen.

Quickly I checked his inventory for a sign of either the forgery or the Monet painting I was searching for. I found nothing. In a corner, I found some very pleasant paintings. Landscapes, still lifes, portraits—all with an Impressionist feel of their own. They were all about two feet by three feet—the size of the forgery I had seen in the Los Angeles museum. And they were all signed in the bottom-right corner: "A.D."

I left the paint-and-turpentine smell and went back through the mildew smell to the fried-grease smell, back into the backyard.

One thing I was sure of: Albert Durant was not in the house—unless he was in the garbage disposal.

I paused a moment in the backyard to let my eyes adjust to the bright sunlight.

The yard sloped down, and between the trees there was a glorious view down the mountain—not of Zurich, but the bucolic outskirts. It was so peaceful and refreshing I decided to stay awhile. Durant might come back.

Then it struck me for the first time—maybe the fleeing man *was* Durant. Though, from the back, anyway, he did not fit the sparse description Jane had given me.

I strolled down the backyard in the hope of finding a

chair or bench to set a spell and await something to carry me on to the next chapter.

I didn't find a bench. I found him, instead. Albert Durant.

Face down.

12

My first thought was to run like firecrackers. Whoever put him there could certainly put me in the same position. Then I realized, if anyone wanted me there, there I would be.

I advanced, cautiously, closer. The body wasn't moving. The arms were outstretched, as though he had been crucified on a cross and fallen on his face. I didn't see any blood. Maybe he died of natural causes—or was only unconscious.

I stepped in the space between his outstretched right arm and his body to get a closer look.

In life he must have carried over two hundred pounds, with the height of a man who would be better served with fifty pounds less.

His kinky salt-and-pepperoni hair looked like someone attempted to give him an Afro and failed. He was wearing his painting clothes and the turpentine smell was probably a blessing, for from the look of his abode and the look of his person, Albert Durant was not a guy who put much stock in bathing.

Suddenly I felt a stunning blow and the next thing I knew I was on the ground next to Albert Durant. Only his right arm wasn't outstretched anymore, it was encircling my legs and he was grinning in my face.

He doesn't brush his teeth either.

"All right, snoopy," he hissed at me, "what do you

think you're doing?"

"I ha–had an ap–appointment to see Al–Albert Dur–Durant at t–t–ten." Fantastic, I thought. I'd developed a stutter. This was absolutely going to be my last case. If this tub of Crisco took it into his head to roll over on me, I would be crushed to death. Instant table wine.

"Don't get so worked up about it," he said, still lying on his belly, his face tilted toward my face. I tried to get up. He held me down. "I called to cancel. You'll have to come back."

I nodded. That was kings with me. I could certainly live without drawing another stinking breath in this tub's company.

I tried to get up again. No bingo. No blackjack. No craps—that's it, no craps—or is it without dice? Anyway, I wasn't going anywhere in that grip. Albert Durant then serenaded me with his hyena laugh. And believe me, if you haven't heard that, you've never died, or lived and wished you hadn't.

"I just saw a man running through your backyard. You know who it might have been?"

"Don't know. I was sleeping."

"Blue blazer—gray pants. About my height."

He shook his head.

"A cut across the back of his neck, like this." I drew a finger across the back of my neck.

"Is that so?" he grumbled. "Bleeding, was he?"

"No. The scar was healed."

"I'm relieved to hear that," he said. "Now, what do you want?"

Strange, I thought, how uninterested he seemed in an intruder. A man so paranoid about the police claims he could care less about an intruder.

"You don't know anyone who fits that description?"

"No!"

"And it doesn't concern you—an intruder—a complete stranger going through your property? I scared him and he left. What do you think he could have wanted?"

"I've no idea. Now what is it you want with me anyway?" he asked. And when Albert Durant asked, with his raucous, angry, dominating voice, you listened.

"If you'll loosen your grip, I'll show you."

He gave me a squinty-eyed look. Not a trace of trust there. He looked like a man who had outgrown trust. The grip loosened enough so I could reach into my pants pockets and produce the pictures, now badly bent. I showed him the one d'Lacy said was a bad copy, first. Without getting up or even turning over, Durant peered at the picture.

"Crap," he intoned, handing it back.

"You paint it?"

"That's an insult," he made sounds like a pig rooting for truffles. "If I *had* painted it, you wouldn't be asking—it would look exactly like an original."

I showed him the second picture. "Ah," he said approvingly, "that's Monet. I could do that well."

"Did you?" I asked.

"Many times, I'm afraid."

"Did you paint this one?"

"No," he said, then added, "Monet did that one."

"How can you be so sure?"

"Because it looks like an original. I'm the only guy alive who can paint like that. There was really only one other, and he's dead."

"Who's that?"

"Monet!" he said, and gave me a powerful blow to my leg, which raised me off the ground, yelping.

"Look here," I said, "can't we get up and talk like normal people?"

"Ha!" he snorted. "Which one of us would you say is normal?"

He had me there. Certainly I was the closer of the two.

"So where did you get these pictures and what do you want from me?"

"I got them in the United States, and I wanted you to tell me who could have painted them."

"The second one, Monet. The first—any kid in the country with a paintbrush."

"You don't have a forgers' guild?"

"You don't know the first thing about art imperson-ation, do you?"

I admitted he was right. I'd never even heard forgery characterized as art impersonation.

"There are two main types. The nincompoops, who open quotes, copy, close quotes, the masters and make no bones about it. They work by the square centimeter. Ten francs the square centimeter, whatever. A Seeing Eye dog could tell it wasn't the original, there is really no need for them to sign their own names to the crap, but they do any-way—'just to be safe.'" This last he spun with a prissy accent, as though this were an occupation only for girls, and boys who aspired to be girls.

He fell silent, as though he'd forgotten he told me there were two types. I reminded him.

"Of course, I'm the second. The true artists who can paint every bit as good as the masters themselves. These men are truly masters in their own right."

"That's you," I acknowledged, "but are there oth-ers?"

"With varying degrees. Some of the others might fool the dilettantes. Guys like Armand Hammer, when he was still kicking, and a bunch of others who can be blinded by a bargain. They see what they want to see—believe what they want to believe. I'm the only one that can fool the best curators in the world."

"And you could have painted this?" I said, holding up the Monet.

"Absolutely."

"But you didn't?"

"No."

"No one else could have? It's that good?"

"Correct."

"Are you acquainted with Franklin d'Lacy?"

He shrugged his shoulders on the ground. He still

made no attempt to get up. He seemed to like it face down on the ground. The sun was bright and it did have a slight enervating effect. "Los Angeles. Everyone knows Franklin—he's the highest profile museum director in the world. A genius at self-promotion."

"Could you fool him?"

He frowned. "If anyone could, it would be me," he said finally. "You know, from what I hear about d'Lacy, he knows his art. He's a real huckster and a circus schlockmeister, but underneath all that bluster is a lot of art savvy. I think I could fool anybody—but I'd expect d'Lacy to be my toughest sell."

"You any idea who might have pulled a switch in London—the fake for the real?"

"That what happened?"

"d'Lacy supervised the packing himself. The crate arrives in Los Angeles with a different painting. Who could have taken the original and what would they do with it?"

He started to sit up—then dropped back down. He still held me in place. I don't know why he thought I wanted to leave—he's the one who claimed he didn't want to see me. Not only was he seeing me, he was keeping me prisoner. "Look," he said, "there are a lot of crooks in the world. This business is no exception."

"I guess you yourself have been considered one of those crooks."

Now, as if involuntarily, Durant sat up and released his grip on me. Then he stood over me as a Buddha, filling his lungs with indignation. "I am not a crook," he said.

From my vantage point, still on the ground, this seemed a most humorous declaration indeed. I let out a stupid laugh.

He kicked me—I jumped out of the way and to my feet. "Hey!" I yipped.

"Don't call me a crook. I'm an artist. I don't scam, I copy. A Xerox machine makes copies. Does anyone go to jail because of it?"

"But don't you pass your work off as original? Isn't

that why you go to jail?"

"Once!" He thrust up a finger. "Only once." He brought his finger down and peered into my face, as if seeing it for the first time. "Say, you aren't from the police, are you?"

"Come on," I said. "Jane made the appointment, remember?"

"Well, Jane is police," he said as if I knew it.

"What?"

"You heard me."

"I can't believe it."

"Why not? You a chauvinist or something? This is a liberated country."

"Hey, she said she was a model."

"Did she now?"

"And there are pictures of her modeling all over the house."

"Really?" He was mocking me.

"I don't get it. You're paranoid about the police, yet your girlfriend is police?"

"All the more reason, eh?" he said, throwing a broad wink in my direction.

I could not believe it. Why would she have lied to me? What could she gain?

"What kind of police work does Jane do?" I asked.

"Art fraud," he said, and treated me again to the hyena laugh.

"You're putting me on."

"Ask her."

"Is she really your girlfriend?"

He wavered his hand in that so-so motion.

"So, why...?"

"Good to keep an eye on the enemy, don't you think?"

I couldn't think.

"Well," he said, "I'd like to invite you in. I wasn't expecting company."

"I'm not company. But, I'd like to see your paintings."

"I don't show my paintings to anyone," he said.

"Why not? I hear you are a great painter."

"Yes, but my great paintings get me in trouble."

"No, I don't want to see the forge...the copies, I want to see yours."

"Mine?" He scrunched his brow as though the message wasn't going to the brain. "What do you mean, *mine*?"

"Your own originals. I hear they are quite good."

He stared, his suspicion aroused. "Mine? Who told you I had original work?"

"Just about everybody. You are quite well-known, you know."

He watched me like a mother hen, as if trying to cut through a line. "They tell you I never sold one of my own?"

"Yes," I said, then added, "neither did Van Gogh in his lifetime." I could tell that pleased him, though he tried to pass it off.

"And my copies bring millions?" he said.

"Yes."

He nodded as though the question was answered, just not satisfactorily.

"Well—may I see them?"

"Maybe another time."

"I'm going back to London."

"You are?"

"Nothing for me here. I came to see you. You say you didn't paint either picture and you have no idea who did."

"Wrong!" he snapped. "I told you Monet painted the good one."

"So you did," I conceded. "So I guess if you won't allow me to see your works of genius, I'll be on my way. I've never met an artist who passed up a sale before, but..."

"Sale? Sale! What do you mean?"

"I thought I might buy an original. A legitimate work of the world's premier painter."

Now he looked right through me and his jaw hung slack. "Sale," he muttered, and shook his head.

The next thing I knew, he was hobbling into the house—he walked like a man who had had a stroke.

I followed him in through the kitchen door. He moved like in a trance. "Maid's on sabbatical," he said, but we moved right on into his studio. "Pile's over there." He waved at the stack of canvases I had perused before. Then he turned his back to me as though he were afraid of my reaction.

I oohed and ahed as I leafed through the work. "This is quite good," I'd mutter, then, "This one is *great*!"

He started to turn around but checked himself at the last moment. I picked out three paintings. They seemed to me now as a cross between Impressionism and Abstract. Like the Monet of the London lights, with less discernible background. "How much for these?" I asked.

He turned slowly and didn't take his eyes off me to look at the canvases I had pulled out.

"Five francs each," he snapped.

"Now..."

"What do you want to pay?" he snorted, as though I had just angered him with a ridiculously low offer.

"Fair market," I said.

"What's market for the unmarketable?" he chortled. He went out of his way to be unpleasant.

I suggested a price in Swiss francs, equivalent to about $1,000 for one, $1,600 for two, or $2,100 for three. He took the $2,100 without even looking at the paintings I had selected.

But after I paid him he seemed to melt. He sat down on his painting stool and cried like a baby.

It seemed like it took forever for him to regain control of himself. When I saw the storm of tears subsiding, I said:

"Did you ever run across a London art dealer named Jacques Moran?" I asked.

"Sure, how could I forget him?" he said. "What with that ugly scar across the back of his neck."

13

My recovery from this bombshell was embarrassingly slow. I decided not to call Durant's attention to his insouciant reaction when I had asked outside about the man with the blue blazer and the neck scar.

"What do you know about Jacques Moran?" I asked him.

"He's a dealer," he shrugged, as though that would excuse a lot of aberrant behavior.

"Honest?"

"A dealer," he said. "How honest can you be?"

"Would you trust him?"

"I have," he said.

"Did he deliver?"

He nodded.

"Can you tell me about it?"

"Not really. Certain matters of confidentiality, you know."

"But he has sold your work—I mean, your artistic impersonations?"

"I don't know."

"You don't know? Who would know?"

"He would, I should think."

"You mean you sold to him, but you don't know what he did with your work?"

"Exactly," he said. "The less I know, the better."

"What are you working on now?"

He waved his arm at his easel. There was a nightscape with colored lights showing through.

"Are you doing any impersonations?"

He leered at me. I was filtered through his bushy eyebrows. "You know what I can't understand about you?" he asked.

"What?"

"How anyone could hire a guy so ineffectual looking to do detective work."

This from a guy who a few minutes ago cried because I bought three of his paintings. No good deed goes unpunished.

"I work cheap," I said.

"How cheap?" he asked.

"Contingency. No results, no dinero."

"You trying to speak German, pal? Dinero is Spanish."

"You know what it means?"

"Of course I know what it means!"

"Bingo!" I said.

"Well, at that rate, I could hire you for a little investigation of my own."

"Oh, what would that be?" I asked.

He shrugged. He wasn't ready to commit.

"Just remember I'm like a lawyer—the bucket at the end of the rainbow has to be substantial or I don't play the game. I only work the real big-money stuff."

"Who you working for?"

"Can't say. Confidential. Privileged."

"You don't have to say. It's easy to guess."

"Why easy?"

"You showed me your hand with those pictures."

"You know anything about those pictures? Where the original is? Who painted them?"

"I told you who painted the genuine one."

"You know where Jacques Moran is now?"

"No."

"He was just here. When did you see him last?"

He shrugged so often, I was beginning to feel for his shoulder muscles. "I don't think I've seen Jacques for two or three years."

I was beginning to feel like I had stumbled into a loony bin.

"How are you getting back to the city?" he asked.

"You have any buses?"

"There's a streetcar up the hill a couple blocks. But you have these paintings. Why don't I call Jane? She'll come for you."

"Oh, I couldn't trouble her."

"She'll love it—she's got to check in on me once in a while anyway–see I haven't flown the coop or taken a dose of strychnine." He went to the phone and dialed a number from memory. "Jane Eaton, please—Jane, this lump of putty you sent out here needs a ride home. Now." That was all he said.

"Now, if you'll excuse me, I have work to do. I've shot too much of the day already."

"May I stay in here?"

"Certainly not. Make yourself at home anywhere else. And if you get a yen to do any housecleaning, don't let any misguided sense of propriety stop you."

He went over to the easel and stared at his almost completed work. Then he took a brush the size of a house painter's brush, dipped it in a can of white paint and painted broad strokes on the canvas, obliterating his painting.

Oh well, I thought, maybe he's got an inspiration for a Van Gogh.

I took my canvases, each about half my size, and went to the living room, where I parked them while I went outside to breathe some fresh air, and clean my lungs of the musty mildew smell of Durant's villa. Geez, I wondered, does that elegant Jane really consort with this guy? Has she ever stayed in this mess?

The other reason I went outside was to see if I could find any sign of Jacques Moran. But Durant had told me so many whoppers, I couldn't believe anything he said. I decided the craziest of all his pronouncements was that Jane was with the police.

I walked the property, seeing no sign of man or yeast, and was beginning to think I had imagined the whole scene with the man in the blue blazer, when I noticed by the side fence a bush had been trampled, and its brittle branches broken.

The fence was only about three feet high and could easily have been jumped. On the other side, the ground seemed undisturbed, but there were no bushes for the intruder to leave his mark on.

I decided Albert Durant, our master forger, was pretty far out. But not so far out to be completely blasé about an intruder. He must have known he was there. Perhaps that was why he called to postpone our meeting.

Jane was at the front in the sewing machine she used for a car. She hopped out, a cheerful gazelle. She started up the walk and I met her at the door.

"I'll get my paintings—I'll be right out."

"Paintings?" She cocked an eye or two.

"I bought three Durants."

A smile of admiration took hold of her flawless features. "That's *won*derful politics, Gil."

I blushed. She started to come in. I turned to block her way. "He doesn't seem in the mood for visitors," I said. "He's working."

She broke into what I might characterize as an unfeminine laughter. "What are you talking about?" she said. "Albert Durant is the world's leading procrastinator. He would rather do *any*thing than work. Besides, I've got to check on him while I'm here."

I stepped aside. She made her way directly to the studio. "Albert," she sang out. "Oh, Albert, I hear you're working. That's simply the most marvelous news I've had all day."

Out of insatiable curiosity, I followed Jane into Albert's lair. She kissed him on the forehead and inquired, "How's our genius today?"

He grunted without looking at her.

"Got enough food in the fridge?" she asked.

"I'm not hungry," he said. I noticed a different Albert Durant in the company of Jane Eaton. He was like a willful, whimpering child, resentful and recalcitrant under the constricting heel of a stern parent.

"Did you have a nice visit?" she asked him.

Another grunt.

"You sold three paintings. Your *own work*!" she fairly shouted. "I'm so proud of you, Albert."

"You set him up."

"What are you talking about? Of course not. That would be demeaning, Albert. I would never demean you."

"Not much. What is it you call this little arrangement we have?"

"Now, Albert, it's for your own good," she said.

"Some good," he said.

She kissed him on the forehead again. She must have had five or six inches on him. "Well, we had a wonderful day, didn't we? *Three* paintings sold. I see it as a new beginning," she enthused. "Just think, you sold *three*!"

We made our way out toward her car. In the living room I retrieved my paintings, and as we left the house we heard him shout, "He *stole* those paintings."

We had to do some maneuvering to get the three canvases to fit in the back seat of Jane's sewing machine, then we were on our way.

"Well," she said, keeping her eyes on the road, "what did you think of my Albert?"

"Which Albert are you talking about? I must have seen three or four."

She laughed. "He does have his moods. But the way I see it, he's entitled. He's such a genius."

"Yes," I said noncommittally. "He says you're a cop." I didn't give it any particular needle, I just let it roll off my teeth.

She laughed again. "Albert," she said, "is such a liar."

I nodded my agreement. "The question is, is he lying this time?"

I thought I heard a clunking sound, but I could just as well have imagined it.

She turned quiet.

Two can play that sport. I turned quiet too. We rode all the way to her apartment in silence. But it was a silence fraught with thought. You could almost hear the gears grinding. One of us would break the silence. I vowed it was not going to be me.

Jane parked outside her apartment. I reached back for my Durant originals and we hiked in silence into her building, then to her second-floor apartment. Wanting some silent activity inside, I spread out my purchases from Albert Durant. It was then I noticed he—or someone—had switched them. The three I bought were not the three I had.

Then I realized Jane was behind me, looking at the paintings.

"He's quite an artist, isn't he?" she asked. Aha! Since she spoke, I could speak. But I didn't. I felt her soft hand gently stroking my neck. That was more like it.

"You didn't tell me who *you* were working for," she said with a touch of a pout in her voice. She was trying to get off the defensive. But she had a point.

"These are not the pictures I bought from him. He switched them."

She laughed. "Just like Albert. He makes his first sale and he can't part with the stuff. Do you judge what he gave you inferior to what you bought?"

"I don't know that much about art. I liked the ones I picked best, of course."

"I guess Albert did too." She gave a gentler laugh this time, as if not sure I was so happy to have her laughing so much.

"Do you really work for the police?" I asked.

"Who do you work for?"

"Confidentiality..."

She smiled. "Okay, come over here and sit down."

She went to the two-seater couch, sat, and patted the space next to her.

I sat. Wouldn't you?

"All right. I expect I'm going to be giving you more than you give me. Isn't that always the woman's lot though?" She smiled. In my defense, it was not a smile much hardier souls than I could resist. "But, I knew what you were about when you came here. You didn't know about me. Fair enough you want to pout about it. I'm not your enemy. Believe it or not, I'd like to help you."

"So are you a cop?"

She sighed. "Would you call that a hangup on your part?" she said. "If you call the police department and ask for Jane Eaton, they'll tell you you have the wrong number."

"Undercover? Incognito?"

"You—a man in your trade—understands how blabbing about what we do can negate any good we might accidentally do," she said, "but I can talk philosophy with you. Philosophically you understand that law enforcement has a vested interest in getting the big boys. Sometimes we work through littler guys to get the big prize. When we feel a little guy's life could be in danger, we protect him—a dead witness is no witness, and, often, no case."

I nodded.

"In something like art fraud, just hypothetically, understand, we are talking big-bucks crime, against guys who have big bucks and big connections. Conning, defrauding the upstanding members of society evokes outrage in those quarters. If we talk ratios, percentages, relative injuries, we are talking small crimes indeed. The poor bloke in a poor ghetto loses his radio in a stickup, he loses a far greater portion of his wealth than some fat cat who picks up a Renoir oil for a couple million, thinking he has put something over on someone. When he finds out it is the other way around, he is prone to outrage."

I put up my hand, to get a word in hedge-wise. "Let me ask you something. If I'm wrong, tell me. If I'm right, you don't have to say anything. You have some connection to a witness-protection program. Albert Durant is your witness. That's why you play the mother hen. He is just a poor sap genius who is a tool for the greedy, unscrupulous art dealers. He gets perhaps thirty to forty thousand dollars for a piece they sell for millions. So some fat cats got the shaft where they don't like to get it and it's become an international cause célèbre."

Jane Eaton didn't say anything.

14

"Is Jacques Moran one of your principals?"

"Principals?" Jane twisted her pretty face.

"Either a suspect or a complainant?"

"He is known to us," she said. "That's all I can say."

"Do you know where he is?"

"No."

"Could you identify him?"

"Sure. If I couldn't, we have files on every important art dealer in the world."

"What does he look like?"

"Fairly good shape, about your height, perhaps forty-five years old or so."

"Any scars?"

"Oh, you mean the thing on the back of his neck?"

"I saw him, running across Durant's backyard."

"You did?" She frowned. It wasn't news that broke her heart, but it didn't make her happy either.

"Does that surprise you?"

"Not particularly. I think he's done business with Albert over the years."

"Really? Is that generally known?"

"I expect so. Why?"

"I'd heard he was a man of impeccable honesty."

"Really? From whom, pray tell?"

"I'm not at liberty..."

"Ah, your principal. Well, that should give me a

good guess at who you are working for—but it doesn't matter to me. Your goals and mine are not conflicting."

"I'm glad to hear that," I said. "How would you characterize Jacques Moran?"

"As a businessman, a man with an eye for the big buck, who will stay within the law when absolutely necessary. You know, he's never been to jail. Albert has. I'd rather it had been the other way around, but what can you do?"

"What can you?"

"Keep trying."

"You don't mean Albert went to jail for something Moran should have?"

"Maybe—but not at the same time. It was another dealer who bought the work from Albert that time."

"Albert conned him? A dealer?"

"I'm afraid so," she admitted.

"He's that good?"

"You might say, at the production of previously produced great art, he's a genius," she said. "Of course, the larger question is: What is art after all? Great art?"

"You mean, what is it or what should it be?"

"Exactly! It should be an added dimension to life. Let's not kid ourselves, until people have full bellies and a warm place to sleep, they aren't going to give a fig for art. So, in the basest sense, we are talking amusements for the rich. When a man makes a hundred thousand a day, what can he do with his money? Five or ten houses, sure, but that's so much trouble. A Rolls-Royce every day? Tiresome, not to say gauche—but art—ah, there you are setting him apart from the hoi polloi."

"But why the forgeries?"

"Because men like this are insatiable. You don't make this kind of big, big money unless you have in you a ferocious drive to excel, and that rarely limits itself to just one phase of life. Now, the supply of universally acknowledged great art is finite. Much more demand."

"Universally acknowledged?"

"Sure, that's the key. To those who seek the endless

approval of their peers, great art is art that enough people acknowledge is great. That's what shoots the prices up. Now, there is a perception that only Monet can paint like Monet. But it's not true. Of course, most artists are satisfied to struggle away expressing themselves. It has integrity. But what about a guy like Albert? He's got a talent to paint paintings that sell for millions of dollars. All he has to do is make copies—or copy a style. The dealers, intoxicated by dollar signs, will find a market among the super-rich who are salivating to own an original Gauguin or Pissarro."

"And Albert can't even sell his own stuff."

"Of course. No cachet. Names, we want names. We are a celebrity-driven society, but nowhere is it more apparent than the art market. People don't buy art, they buy names."

"So where does the intrinsic merit of the piece fit in?"

"Ah, there is the great question. Albert Durant's copies are intrinsic merit," she said. "If some museum curator in Texas is fooled by a Durant forgery, why shouldn't it command a price commensurate with the originals?"

"I think it should," I said.

"So do I," she agreed. "You see, I'm very sympathetic to him. That's why I'm protecting him."

"What danger is he in?"

"First, he's a danger to himself. He can't keep himself from painting these forgeries. If there were only more good guys like you who would buy his paintings..."

"And have them switched by the artist."

She shook her head. "I'll get your paintings for you. I expect he was only joking."

"So what other danger is he in?" I asked.

"When people do illegal things for very high stakes there is inherent danger. Some disgruntled guy who's been conned may want to pop him—or, more likely, have it done. Guys with those kind of bucks aren't used to being conned. Makes them mad."

"How do they know it's Albert?"

"Small world, the art world, in this price range," she said. "Word gets out."

"Do you think you could tell Albert's work—pick it out in a roomful of originals or from a photograph?"

"It's my field."

I showed her the photographs I had of the two paintings d'Lacy claimed had been switched. The ones Albert Durant denied painting.

She looked at them only briefly.

"He painted both of them," she said.

15

All well and not so good, I'm thinking. A lot of evidence makes me suspicious of the guy who is supposed to pay me my million. I'm in a self-defeating mode. There has to be some way to get out of this rut. If I were at home I'd stroll among my cycads and palms, looking for signs of incipient leaves, marveling in the sign of new life in those painfully slow plants. In time of stress I missed my garden more.

I looked back at Jane, beside me on the tight couch. "Albert Durant swears this picture is a Monet original." I showed her the "good" painting.

"Tsk, tsk," she said. "I wonder why."

"You mean he'd lie about that?"

"Would you lie to a stranger for a hundred thousand American dollars?" she asked me.

"But isn't he proud of being able to fool experts?"

"All right, take your choice: pride before a stranger or a hundred thou? I should clarify that. He's really shilling for fifty thou. He got fifty for delivering the picture. He gets another fifty if it passes muster for a year after it is recovered by the museum."

"But it hasn't been recovered, has it?"

She pasted those model's eyes on me and I decided they looked more like a policewoman's eyes after all. She caught me, and while she wasn't going to gloat, she wanted to make sure I realized she knew.

"Apparently not," she said.

"Do you know where it is?" I asked.

"What's in it for me?" she wondered aloud.

"What do you want?"

"Cooperation."

"Cooperation? On what? I don't know anything that would help you. I don't even know anything yet that will help me."

"You do too. And with my help you will know a lot more. Why, I've certainly helped you already."

"I don't know." I frowned. "I'm not absolutely convinced that the guy you said painted these would lie to *me* about it. Why, I bought three paintings from him—his first three. And he was so happy, he cried."

"Did he really?" She was such a skeptic. "How sweet. This is the same guy who switched paintings when you weren't looking? Was that an act of honesty?"

I worked my flat hand down from my forehead, over my eyes, nose and mouth, in an unconscious attempt to wipe away the weariness. "Maybe not," I conceded.

"That's the thing about life," she mused, "you have to make choices. Who do you trust here—Albert—or me?"

"Well, he was a lot more open than you were about what you do. Five a.m. for a modeling session!"

"Oh, but that was true. I'll show you the proofs when I get a set."

"Two jobs?"

"You could say that."

"Darn it." I slapped the arm of the couch, trying to show what a forceful personality I really was. "There you go again with the mystery stuff."

"Okay, I'll make you a deal," she said.

"What kind of a deal?"

"I'll come clean with you, if you do the same with me."

"Hey, what is this? I don't get you. Does Sarah know you're a cop?"

"Sarah knows what I do."

"And yet she sent me to you?" I shook my head but

it didn't clear it any. "I can't imagine what she had in mind."

"You asked to get to Albert, I believe. I'd say she did you a favor." She twinkled those model/cop eyes at me. "Of course, maybe you would rather not have met me."

"My dear Jane," I said with my profound voice, "not meeting you would have been a tragedy of the first rain."

"First rain? What does that mean?" she asked. "Oh," it came to her, "you mean first water. Cute."

And she was too. Maybe "beautiful" would have been more accurate.

"Let me ask you something," she said. "Don't answer any more than you care to. Is your fee is contingent on the return of the painting? If so, would you be willing to play ball with me, if I got you the painting?"

"Ball?"

"Just an expression. You would not have to cooperate until you saw the painting."

"How will I know it's the same?"

"You have the photograph," she said.

"Albert could easily forge one from that."

"He already did. This is Albert's Monet we are talking about. The good one."

"Can you get him to say that to me?"

"Are you kidding? I can get Albert to tell you he's Santa Claus."

"That's just it. I can't trust him."

"But you can trust me."

How, I wondered, could she be so sure? She was locking me in her steely eyed gaze. I don't even remember what color her eyes were—blue, hazel, pink? They were just sort of dreamy. That may have been the first time I realized saying "no" to this beauty was not in the deck for me.

The bimbo is trying to turn me, I thought. How did I get myself into this? The easiest thing would be to get out of here, fast. But my goal is the Monet with question marks, and she claims to have it—or know where it is.

But if she did, why wouldn't she just seize it and lock it in a vault somewhere?

Could it have been buried under all that trash at Albert Durant's house? I looked, but, of course, how could you?

"So, I have to make some calls," I said, standing up. I considered leaning over to kiss her but decided she had ulterior motives romancing me, and I was beginning to feel used.

"You may make them here," she said, waving to the phone.

I smiled.

"Oh, I'll leave if you like." She stood too.

"Not necessary. All those numbers turning up on your phone bill? Not too brilliant."

"Oh, suit yourself," she said, a bit put out. "My offer is really a favor to you. I know almost as much as you do about what you are doing and for whom. By the time my phone bill comes, I'll know more than you do."

She was probably right. "All the same, I hope it won't hurt your feelings if I hang on to a little privacy."

"Suit yourself," she said, flapping her elbows like a bird. She started to gather her things for an exit.

"Before I make my calls, may I make sure I understand what you are offering?"

She straightened from bending over to pick up her purse—stood, and waited. Didn't nod, didn't say "Yes."

I inhaled with a huff. "If I tell you who I am working for and what I'm trying to accomplish, you will tell me who you work for, what your goals are and will give me the painting to take to the U.S."

Her smile was the smile of conquest. "*Loan* you the painting to take to the U.S."

"Well, that's okay with me, but how will you get it back? I can't be responsible for that."

"Of course not. I'll bring it back."

"How will you do that?"

"Simple—I'm going with you."

"Oh." I was staggered by the thought. I guessed that if Franklin d'Lacy saw Jane, he'd forget about the painting.

"Okay," I said, "I'll think it over. I'll let you know at dinner."

"I'm sorry, I won't be able to have dinner with you tonight. I have a date."

"Oh?" I must have looked shocked, because she said:

"You didn't think I was the Virgin Mary or something?"

"I..." I stammered. "Would you like me to move out for the night?"

"Oh, no, we'll go to a hotel."

"Oh... Are you sure I'm not in the way?"

"Not at all. I never use my home."

"Use?"

"I'm sorry, that was indelicate. I never bring my Johns back here."

"Johns?"

"Dates."

"Is this modeling business or police work?"

She laughed. And the thing that was so strange about her laugh was that it was so wholesome. Maybe she was putting me on. Making me jealous so I would go for her proposition.

"Well, maybe I'll go back to London tonight. We can talk later."

"I wouldn't do that if I were you," she said, and I resented her getting possessive—especially under the circumstances.

"Oh, why not?" I was defensive.

"Because the 'Monet' is here, not in London."

I analyzed my position. My agreement with d'Lacy was to return the painting, not authenticate it. If it was a five-dollar forgery, I had earned my million. (Six hundred and change, net.) But hey, I should get a tax man. Maybe for the extra four hundred grand I could become a citizen of the Cayman Islands or something. Time to look into that later.

Before I decided whether or not to offer Jane a deal, I'd offer one to d'Lacy.

"Let me think about it," I muttered. I hadn't realized she had gone into the bedroom. I dropped back on the couch and fell into the thinking mode. But I resolved nothing except to give it another day in Zurich. It was a nice town anyway. I missed my palm trees, but I could take a little more of Zurich. Especially if the "Monet" really was here.

I heard her before I saw her. It was the high-heeled click of stiletto spikes on her hardwood floor. I looked down at the floor, attracted to the noise, and discovered for the first time the tiny circular impressions in the wood, which were undoubtedly caused by these ridiculous shoes. My eyes followed her lithe, perfect, model's body upward—the long, black-mesh-stockinged legs disappearing into a velveteen skirt the color of Franklin d'Lacy's rosewood desk, up to a pure-white cashmere sweater that looked untouched by human hands. The whole ensemble had been applied in record time with a paint-spray gun, and from the neck down she was a knockout.

Her body was like one of those stretched out on a Caribbean beach in a stretch swimsuit—in travel sections for newspapers the world over. These idealistically proportioned bodies were meant to set the boys adrooling and loosen the purse strings for a winter schlepp to the sunshine.

The girl wouldn't be there, of course. She was here in this apartment in Zurich, Switzerland, and I was staring at her like I had sunstroke. It was when my eyes got above the neck that I had my trauma.

Jane had ladled on so much makeup that she looked like a two-dollar hooker, while south-of-the-border prices were bound to run considerably higher.

Her blond hair was piled up in a beehivey arrangement that went more with the makeup than the clothes.

Why, I wondered, did women paint their faces so drastically? Was it possible there were men who actually liked them that way? I decided there had to be, because I was sure Jane Eaton knew her business.

"Ta ta," she said, wiggling her fingers at me. "I'll see you in the morning." And she was out the door with the ample skin of some dead animal in hand.

What a world. You just never could tell anything about a person.

Then I decided she might be on an undercover mission. But how could she be? Certainly she would stand out like a sore finger in that getup—and I don't think the Swiss went in for prostitution entrapment.

The more I thought all this over, the less sense it made to me.

For starters, Albert Durant, erratic resident eccentric, is supposed to be in such grave danger that the police have hidden him away in their equivalent of our witness-protection program. But he doesn't seem hidden at all. Jacques Moran knows where he is and, according to the scenario I am being fed, Jacques may constitute the greatest danger. Then he is all alone there. No one "protecting" him. Jane goes out now and again to look in on him, but that's no protection.

Jane claims both pictures are fakes, both painted by Albert Durant. Albert stoutly denies painting either of them—is insulted to have the second attributed to him, though he admits he could have done the Monet as well as Monet.

Why is Moran in Switzerland, and why is he out schmoozing with Durant?

Does Jane really know where the painting is? And *if* she does know, *why* does she?

Was the painting really switched? If so, by whom, and why? If the police (Jane) know where it is, it isn't likely it could be resold.

It just looked to me like everybody was scamming everybody else.

So where did that put me vis-à-vis that million? I'd better get on the trumpet and call d'Lacy.

Fun as this expedition was, it was starting to eat away at my first fee, and the chances of connecting with the second fee seemed to be receding.

Jane had me so brainwashed I actually picked up her phone to call LAMMA's director, Franklin d'Lacy. Then I

112

came to my senses and went for a walk to clean my muddled mind and settle on my last-gasp plan for enriching my bank balance six hundred grand, net.

I put the call through at a phone in the Grand Hotel lobby, looking out at the lake. So many fantastic lakes in Switzerland. All that melting snow has to go someplace. It was just four o'clock—seven in L.A. I put d'Lacy to the test. Did he really start his day at seven?

"Gil, Gil, about time. What's it been, two days?"

"One day. Good, though. A productive day."

"I hope so. They are just about to spring the trap here," he said, sucking in the air of conspiracy. "What have you got?"

"I think I've found it."

"*Fantastic*!" He was quite enthused. "When can you get it here?"

"Depends."

"On what?" He turned suspicious.

"You know I'm no art expert, so I don't want to be flimflammed."

"You won't be."

"But what if I produce the picture and you decide it's a copy?"

"Well, I'm not paying for a copy. I hope you understand that. What good would...?"

"I do," I said. "But reasonable people can differ. I'm not risking my life for a fee I may never see, if the work is not acceptable to you for any reason."

"Gil," he pleaded, "why all this sophistry? Do you have the Monet or not?"

"I have what I think is your painting, or rather I know where it is."

"Where?"

"Sorry. My fee, you know. Now, it is not going to be a piece of pie getting it to L.A. First I have to have your guarantee in writing that this is your purchase. I will have my picture taken with it, and we will blow it up to life size if you like. You say yea or nix. If it's yea, the million will have to go into an escrow account in your name and mine with irrevocable instructions that when I deliver the work to you we be photographed with it, and the photo be blown to life size to compare with the original."

"Oh, Gil, what a lot of falderal. Whatever happened to old-fashioned trust? I'm a substantial man in the community. Isn't my reputation worth anything?"

"Sure, but more to you than to me, I'm afraid. I can see how easy it would be to do me out of my million. Nobody wants to pay a fee, and that includes you and me. As for old-fashioned trust, something must have happened to it, or I wouldn't be over here trying to get your painting back."

"Are you in London?"

"No."

"Where are you?"

"Somewhere else."

"Oh, Jesus, Gil, you really live this cloak-and-dagger stuff, don't you?"

"When I'm trying to satisfy a principal, in this case you, I guess you could say I live it. Day and night."

"Very nice, except I think now you are trying to satisfy your lust for that million."

He had me there, big time.

"Have you located Moran?"

"Not exactly," I said. "I think I've seen him—so I'm pretty sure he's alive. But I haven't spoken to him."

"Have him authenticate the Monet. I'll take his word for it."

That stopped me. I didn't like the sound of it. It was as full of loopholes as a ton of Swiss cheese, but if I could waylay Jacques Moran, it could be an efficient solution. "Fax that to me with your signature," I said. "Now, can you cough up the million or not?"

"I told you before, you get that..."

"Huh-uh," I interrupted the old spiel. "See if you can work the escrow. I'll call you back tomorrow. But no tickie, no pickie," I said and hung up. Getting tougher, I thought. But tough *enough* remained to be seen. I realized I was pushing a desperate man. A man who most likely did not have a million dollars. Pushing him to further desperation. On the other hand, I wasn't willing to risk my life for pistachios.

16

Wrung out from my telephone encounter with Franklin d'Lacy, I decided to call Sarah in London. It would soothe me.

I decided (1) I missed her. (2) Seeing Jane go out looking like a bimbo made me miss Sarah more. (3) I wondered what hidden part Sarah might have in this quadruple scam.

I never liked to talk on those wall phones in airports and hotel lobbies—it was impossible to guarantee privacy. I talked low, but then couldn't be heard. Especially these foreign connections. But here in the hotel I had semiprivacy and most of these people didn't speak my language.

Sarah answered the phone, cheerfully identifying her gallery. "This is Sarah," she said, "I would be pleased to be of service." The British were so gracious. When you asked a London bobby where something was, he took you to it. In New York you are lucky to be pointed in the right direction.

"Hi, Sarah, it's Gil Yates."

"Oh, Gil, so nice to hear your voice."

"Likewise."

"How did you find Jane?" she asked. At first I didn't understand what she meant, and I was about to say "At the airport."

But then I caught on. I often do. "Interesting, Sarah. Very interesting. How much do you know about Jane?"

"A bit. We're pretty good friends."

"Do you know what she does for a living?"

"Sure."

"All her jobs?"

"What do you mean, all? She's a model."

"What sort of 'model' do you mean?" I put the right inflection on the key word so no one would misunderstand my meaning.

"Fashion, I suppose," Sarah said. "She's been on magazine covers, why?"

"Does she work for the police?"

"Police? I don't think so."

"Does she do any of her modeling at night—in hotel rooms with gentlemen she refers to as Johns?"

Sarah began laughing. "Oh, Gil," she said, "Jane is such a tease. I'm very much afraid she has put you on a bit."

"You should have seen, and smelled, her leaving her apartment this afternoon. Told me she'd be back in the morning. Had a date with a John was how she put it. Made up like a two-quid whore."

"Oh, dear." Sarah said. "I did tell you she had a thing with Albert Durant, didn't I?"

"Yes..."

"Well, I expect that's where she is. Her 'John,' as you say. I'm afraid she's not a two-quid hooker, though I wonder how you would know what they look like." She giggled. "Not to *mention* inflation."

"How about a two-hundred-quid hooker? A thousand?"

"Oh, dear, no—not Jane. I'm very much afraid there's some misunderstanding."

"Misunderstanding?" I said. "This whole fiasco is one great misunderstanding."

"How do you mean?"

"Nothing is as it seems. Everything I am told by one person is contradicted by the next."

"Isn't that life though," she said as in agreement. I had asked her to check periodically with the Westpark

117

Agency, who were watching for Jacques Moran.

"No Moran. But today, there was a new visitor."

"Any description?"

"Expensively dressed. Not too tall. Dark hair. Swarthy looking."

"Any idea who it is?"

"I've not."

I stood back from where I was leaning against the phone wall, to stretch. When I did, I caught sight of a man entering the hotel who looked very much like Jacques Moran. "Sarah," I said quickly, "I think I see Moran."

"There in Zurich?"

"Yes—gotta go—call you later."

I hung up and hurried to intercept the gentleman as he stepped to the elevator.

"Mr. Moran?" I inquired. "Jacques Moran?"

He looked at me with sunken eyes that told me he was neither well-rested nor happy to be recognized.

"Do I know you, sir?" he asked in a polite but wary British accent.

"We have many mutual friends."

"Oh?"

"I'd like to talk to you for a few minutes if I might."

"I'm terribly sorry, I'm late for an appointment upstairs."

"I won't take long," I said.

"Sorry." He had a grim smile on his face as he shook his head.

Up close, Jacques Moran looked what we would call "veddy British." Dressed to impress in dark worsteds, a crackling clean shirt and solid navy tie, he had a face lined with worry. And from the look of them, the lines were a recent encumbrance to a successful, substantial-looking man.

The elevator door opened and he nodded his farewell and got in—I followed. He looked distressed. "Look here, I don't know you, I don't want to talk to you, I don't mean to be rude, but you can't come up with me."

"Oh, is this your private elevator?" I was trying to

make like a guest in the hotel. But he realized that.

"Are you a hotel guest?" he asked.

"I have information on a painting you seem to be looking for." The doors closed.

"What painting?" he asked with a mixture of hope and suspicion.

"The one you're looking for."

His shoulders slumped. Jacques Moran seemed to dissolve in my presence.

"Shall we go to the lobby or the bar to talk about it?" I asked.

"No, would you mind? Come to my room." He worked the buttons and we were off on floor five. I followed him down the hall and fixed my stare on his neck scar. His movements were less fleet than when he was leaving Albert Durant's backyard.

He opened the door to his room and stood aside for me to precede him. The better sense of going in before a stranger gave way to his British manners.

I went into a simple European hotel room in a deluxe hotel. I expected a suite for a man involved in a six-teen-million-dollar sale. Instead, there was a chair, a small table and a bed. He insisted I take the chair. He sat on the bed.

"Now, suppose you tell me who you are?"

"I'm Gil Yates," I said, "from the United States." Since I'd never said that before, I hadn't realized it rhymed, and I giggled.

"It rhymes," I said. Moran glared at me.

"And your interest in this 'painting'?"

"I'm talking about a Monet sold to the Los Angeles Museum, but not delivered. That ring any chimes with you, Mr. Moran?"

He looked blank—like he was reliving a nightmare. He took a deep breath, then let the air just fizzle out. "You say you know where the painting is?"

"Yes," I lied. So, okay, I thought, maybe what I said was not strictly true, and if it was true, it couldn't be backed up with any convincing documentation. Not yet.

"So what's your game?" Jacques Moran asked. He looked so pathetic on that lonely bed. "Money?"

"No, I've been hired to get it back."

"By Hadaad?"

I was shocked, but tried not to let on.

"Or d'Lacy?" he said. "Or has the museum got wind of it by now?"

"I'm not at liberty to explain my association. Suffice it to say, my goals match yours. If I'm not mistaken about your goals?"

He volunteered nothing. He looked like he was just too weary of the whole thing.

"All right," I said, "here's my understanding of your situation. You sold the Monet in good faith, or not in good faith, to d'Lacy. He claims he didn't get it. He, or his buddy Hadaad, is out for your skin if you don't produce the right painting. Am I right so far?"

He just stared at me through eyes that seemed to get blearier by the minute.

"So tell me why you want the painting," I said. "Maybe I can put you in touch with the person who has it."

At that, I thought his look turned from pity to pitiful. "Who has it?"

I spread my palms, meaning he'd have to give me more before I told him.

He didn't understand it that way. If he did understand, he didn't like it. "Listen, my man, don't play with me." Still he was more weary than angry. "I've been through too much. My reputation is at stake, my life is in danger. People I trusted screwed me."

"Trusted?"

"Certainly!" he snapped. "You cannot live without some trust. You ship a painting by a carrier you used for twenty-some years. You trust them to protect it and deliver it."

I nodded. "Okay," I said, willing to agree to a point, "but what were you doing at Albert Durant's place this morning?"

He looked perplexed. "Albert Durant?" he asked. "The art forger? Is he in town?"

"You mean, you weren't there this morning?"

"There? Where is there?"

"At Durant's villa."

"I've no idea what you are talking about."

"You don't know Durant?"

"Not personally. I know who he is."

"Never done business with him?"

"Certainly not!"

"He says you have."

"He's wrong."

I tried to do a take of Moran's face. If he was lying, it seemed to me he had convinced himself. But hadn't I seen the neck scar with my own eyes? True, he was dressed differently than this morning... "May I look in your closet?"

"Why?" I understood his suspicion.

"Do you have a blue blazer?"

"No."

"May I verify that by looking in your closet?"

He waved his hand at me in disgust. I got up and pawed through his suits in the room closet. No blue blazer.

"Could be at the cleaners," I said.

"I have nothing at the cleaners." He pointed to the phone. "Why don't you call and ask them?"

"Are you registered under your own name?"

"Oh, this is getting a bit too much. Whose name would I be registered under?"

"My apologies," I said. "I must have mistaken someone else for you. It was the scar on the back of your neck."

He put his hand there, automatically, as if to see if it were still there. "I'd actually forgotten the scar," he said. "I imagine others have them."

"How did you get yours?"

"Nothing dramatic. I didn't cheat the guillotine at the last moment. It was a childhood mishap. Put my head through a window, then, in a stupid reaction, tried to stand up suddenly and I sliced my neck with the broken edge."

"I'm sorry."

"Oh, I'm not self-conscious anymore. Was in my youth. Everyone asked what it was. I didn't fancy the attention. For some years I let my hair grow to cover it. Now I don't bother. Since my hair went gray it looked so stupid long."

I was beginning to wonder if someone might have been trying to impersonate him at Durant's, so I asked him.

"I've no idea."

"Any idea why anyone would want to do that?"

"Not offhand."

"If you let your imagination run free, what kind of scenario could you come up with—someone who wanted me to see a guy I thought was you at Albert Durant's?"

"I've no idea, really."

"Someone who wants me to believe the Monet was a forgery? But he probably was in cahoots with Durant—they were there at the same time—and Durant swears it's an original."

"He claims he is the only forger in the world who could paint as well as Monet and he didn't paint it. Ergo, it must be a Monet."

"Well, he's got a good opinion of himself," Moran said. "I can't say he isn't right."

"Do you know another forger who could have painted the Monet in question and fooled you?"

His eyebrows were in a bind. "Durant's wrong. There are other good forgers. We all like to believe we can't be fooled. But we all live in fear of being fooled—sticking our neck out and having it chopped off."

"Can you name some other forgers who could fool you?"

"Not offhand. I don't deal with forgers."

"Ever been tempted?"

"No."

"Ever have anyone fool you with a forgery that you represented as an original?"

"No."

"How can you be sure?"

"The forgeries are smoked out eventually. Skeptics abound in our business. There is always a regiment of doubters ready to pounce on any new discovery. They are often right, but not always."

"You are convinced what you sold LAMMA is a genuine Monet?"

"Absolutely."

"Couldn't be wrong?"

"Not about that," he said. "If it were a forgery, why would anyone have stolen it?"

"Couple reasons come to mind. One, they could have been fooled into thinking it *was* original, and two, it would make it seem, by virtue of the theft, as you suggest, indisputably original, of outlandish value; and at the same time, being missing, would not have to bear the scrutiny of the experts."

"Oh, I don't know..."

"What better way to fool the insurance company?"

"Is that who you work for?"

"Sorry, can't say," I said. "What a nice way to get sixteen million, without producing the body."

"There are, if I may say so, a few things wrong with that hypothesis. The first is no insurance company is going to pay anything to anybody without establishing beyond a doubt that the money was paid in the first place in an arm's-length transaction." He shifted his legs and the bed squeaked.

"You were paid?"

"Certainly. And the records are all there. The money is in the bank."

"So you could just return the money?"

"Except I paid for the painting."

"Who did you pay?"

"Phillipe Rogier."

"And that can be traced through the bank records?"

"Certainly."

"Would you give me access to those records?"

"If you produce your *bona fides.*"

"I will ask my principal permission to disclose his or her interest."

"His or her?" He smiled ruefully. "A politically correct shamus. I'm most impressed. Of course, I always felt the generic 'he' was more than satisfactory."

"Can you tell me one more thing?"

"Perhaps," he said cannily.

"What part does Michael Hadaad play in this shenanigan?"

"A rather unfortunate characterization, I'm afraid," Jacques Moran said from his diminutive perch on the edge of the bed. "Michael Hadaad made the transaction possible at the buying end by supplying enough cash to supplement what the museum paid."

"How much was that?"

"I don't know."

"You don't know what you were paid?"

"Of course I do. Sixteen million dollars—about eleven million pounds sterling. I don't know how much of it was Hadaad's."

"A guess?"

"I don't guess. If I had to speculate, I'd say from a quarter to a half that amount." He thought a moment. "But I could be way off."

"Is he associated with you in any other way?"

Jacques Moran looked deeper into my eyes. Now I was going over the line, his stare seemed to say. "I don't know that you have any legitimate need to delve further into my affairs. When can I see the painting?"

"Again, I must check with my principal."

"Fair enough. Where can I get in touch with you?"

"I'll call you," I said. I stood and he followed. We shook hands. "Oh, by the way," I said, "how do you happen to be looking for the painting in Zurich?"

"Anonymous tip," he said. Then he smiled at me. "A pretty good one, apparently."

On my way out I went to the house phone—I picked it up and asked the operator for Jacques Moran. She rang the room. When he picked up the phone, I hung up.

I called the laundry. "This is Moran in five-twelve. I'm embarrassed to say I can't remember whether or not I left my blazer with you."

"Five-twelve, you say? I'll be happy to check for you, Mr. Moran. One moment, please." When she came back on the line, she said, "I'm sorry, sir, we don't seem to have anything for you. Would you like us to pick up something?"

"Oh, no, thanks. I'll call later."

Out in the street, I realized that the big challenge here was going to be knowing who to believe—preferably the person who was telling the truth—if anyone was.

I drew in a year's supply of Swiss air, and mused at what a treat it was for a Torrance, California, boy to be standing on the super-clean streets of this wonderful city, enjoying what came as close to a perfect day of any I've lived.

When my mind is on something important, I am a fairly oblivious guy. I stepped into the street without paying too much attention. Sure, I saw cars, but it didn't occur to me that one of them might want to run me down. Not until I heard the engine roar and I looked in that direction to see this big black machine bearing down on me like a bullet from the gun of a crack marksman.

I jumped about a mile and managed to get away with a nick in my thigh and bruises from my fall in the gutter in front of a parked car.

I was so stunned, the best I could do was crawl to the curb as the car sped away. I managed to pull myself up into a sitting position on the curb and sat there holding my head in my hands.

In London, forty people would have asked if I wanted help.

In Zurich, no one stopped.

17

When I'd recovered my senses, I stood up and found a cab at the motor entrance to the hotel. I decided walking the streets of Zurich, for the time being, was not for me.

I got in the cab and gave him Albert Durant's address. He looked it up in his map book, and we were off. I settled back in the seat and closed my eyes. Then I began to wonder for the first time who it was wanted me dead, and why. I decided I didn't know that many people connected to the case who knew where I was and had the means and desire to do me in. Or perhaps it was just a scare. If it was, it was an eminently good one. Jane? Albert Durant? Sarah? Jacques Moran? One less likely than the next. Oh, I suppose Moran could have telephoned someone, but would there have been time? Did he know I stopped to telephone the laundry? The line wasn't busy when I called his room.

It must have been a mistaken-identity thing, or a freak accident.

I wished.

The sun was starting to fade as the taxi wound up the hill. When we got to Durant's villa I saw Jane's sewing machine parked out front.

"We're here," the driver said. "This it?"

"What? Oh, yes," I said. "Yes, it is—thank you. Now could you just take me back to Jane's?"

"Jane's?" the driver asked.

"Oh, yes, of course, sorry," I said, and I gave him

her address.

On the ride back down I was feeling better—a lot better about Jane.

It was dark when I let myself into Jane's apartment. While I was fumbling for the light I thought I heard noises. "Oh, no," I lamented to myself, "not again." I found the switch and threw on the light, with my back to the wall and my finger still on the switch in case I had to suddenly turn it off again. But I seemed to be quite alone.

Stealthily I made my way through the apartment. I was much relieved to find nothing. I flopped down on the love-seat couch and tried to still my pounding heart. When I was close to normal again, I decided to call Sarah at home. I didn't think her number on Jane's bill would stir up a fly's nest.

"Hi, Sarah."

"Oh, Gil, glad you called. I overnighted some Polaroids of the visitor at the Morgan Gallery. You should have them tomorrow."

"Great!"

"When are you coming back?"

"As soon as I get my hands on the painting," I said. "Assuming no one tries to run me down again."

"What's that? Run you down how?"

"With a car."

"Oh, Gil, they didn't? Oh, Gil." She sounded truly miserable.

"You have any ideas?"

"'Fraid not, Gil. But you be careful. I'm afraid at eleven million pounds sterling you are in the big, bad leagues. I think you ought to come back here where I can watch out for you. Nobody tried to hurt you here."

"I think you have a good point."

"No amount of money is worth trading your life for."

I always felt good talking to Sarah. She had a soothing quality—a feather smoother. But after I said goodbye I thought about some things, and decided in light of the threats to my person, it might not be a bad idea to have d'Lacy's phone number appear on Jane's bill. I could always explain it away if things turned out all right. If they didn't turn out all right, it would be a shred of evidence about who my employer was.

I dialed LAMMA, and wrote a note to reimburse Jane for the calls.

I never once had to wait for d'Lacy. I admired him for that. Of course, I did wonder if he didn't have more important work to do, but I guess he didn't. What work could be more important than keeping your job?

"What's new, Gil. Any progress?"

"Quite a bit is new. Progress, that's a matter of definition. I found Jacques Moran."

"You did?" He was hearty in his approbation. "Fantastic! Where? Does he have the painting?"

"Apparently he is looking for it too."

d'Lacy's tone dropped an octave. "I shouldn't wonder," he said. "I hope you gave him hell for me."

"That's one of the reasons I'm calling," I said. "Jacques Moran is pressing me for details of my employment in return for his cooperation. I told him I would have to clear that with my unnamed principal."

"What do you think, Gil?"

"Entirely up to you. I'd like his cooperation, of course."

"If we tell him, do you think you can get him to call me?"

"Try."

"Go for it. He's on our side. At least he *used* to be. You don't think he could be pulling a fast one on us, do you? Instead of looking for the Monet he could be hiding it—or selling it to someone else?"

"In this mess, it's so hard to say," I said. "It's gotten so I don't know who to believe."

"Believe me," d'Lacy said.

"Why?"

"I'm paying you," he laughed.

"Are you?"

"You have nothing to worry about on that score, remember."

"Well, I'm afraid I'm worried. I can deliver the painting, but you can so easily say *I* stole it, or I'm an agent of the thief and have me locked up."

"Oh, Gil—your fantasies are running away with you."

"You think so? I've sunk over ten grand in this expedition so far. I've got to buy a row of seats to get that painting back. If I don't get anything at the other end, I won't be a happy campsite."

"Don't worry."

"I'm worried," I said. "Now, I've had another offer here, so it's going to be up to you. Why don't you come over here and bring the million? We'll take the painting back together."

"You don't understand museum politics," he said. "What other offer have you had?"

"You know I don't talk about my clients."

"Is it related to the painting?"

"Can't say."

"You aren't two-timing me, are you?"

"I'm working for you as long as I can reasonably believe I will get my fee. I'm afraid I have lost all faith in that."

"But why?—Gil. This is ridiculous."

"Is it? Where's the escrow?"

"Gil!" He was pleading now. "You understand I'm not a wealthy man. I don't have a million bucks lying around."

"I understand that. I also understand that when you get the painting you will have the painting but you still won't have the million."

"Gil!"

"Where will it come from?"

"There are ways, Gil, you have to trust me."

"Hadaad is a possibility. Let him put it up. He

wouldn't miss a million."

"Mike's been a brick through this whole thing."

"So I understand."

"What's that supposed to mean, Gil? I'm not sure I like your tone."

"Over here, I've discovered just what a brick he is. Only I'm not sure I'm pronouncing it right."

"Gil!"

"You have any idea who would try to run me down in the streets?"

"What? What are you talking about, Gil?"

"Someone tried to kill me with a car. Now I don't know that many people who even know me here, let alone know what I'm doing. I just thought you might have some ideas."

"Gil, you're nuts. I don't even know where the hell you are. The idea that I'd have someone run you down is stupid. How would I get my painting with you under the wheels of a car?"

"I didn't say you, Franklin," I said. "But have you seen Hadaad lately?"

"Michael wouldn't do that."

"Of course he would."

"Gil! That's uncalled for."

"I'm here. And here is my final offer, as they say in the Mafia."

"Mike Hadaad is not Mafia!"

"I didn't say he was—but it's an interesting idea." I paused for a reaction, but from Franklin d'Lacy came only silence. I let him break it. When he did, his voice was calm and reasoned and even a little engaging.

"Gil," he said, "Michael's been a brick about this whole thing. He put up a lot of the cash in the first place. He wants the painting back. If I'm out of a job, he's out. He doesn't want to be out. We all have large egos."

"I appreciate that, but someone tried to flatten my ego as well as the rest of me, and it might help me to know who that was."

"Are you sure it was deliberate?"

"Sure."

"And that you were the target?"

"Well, he got me—I didn't see anyone else."

"Could have been a mistake."

"And cows could give Pepsi-Cola. It just isn't very likely," I muttered.

"Can't help with that, Gil," he said.

I was still convinced that the dirty hands of Michael Hadaad were in here somewhere. Too many things pointed that way.

First was my own experience with that worthy where he tried to blow my brains to Tahiti rather than pay me an agreed-upon fee that I had most surely earned. And I only got it, in the end, by chicanery, a happenstance he is not liable to forget.

Perhaps I was a trifle naive thinking Hadaad would recommend me for a job with no secret hatchet to grind, no hidden agenda. I am less naive now.

I switched topics. "I met Albert Durant," I said casually.

"Really? Where?"

I ignored that. "I showed him the pictures. He says one is a Monet, the other a fake. Says he didn't paint either of them."

"He knows painting. I've always sort of admired his skill, you know."

"But others insist he painted both of them."

"Others? Who others?"

"Experts," I said.

"Well, when you get the Monet back, show it to them. No expert is going to call that painting a fake."

"You are so confident?"

"Less so about getting it back," he said. "But no way did Durant do the painting I bought. Maybe the fake."

"Albert says the second is sloppy work and far beneath him."

"Well, he should know."

"But suppose a guy of his surpassing skill, a guy who could imitate the masters with aplomb, *tried* to do sloppy work intentionally. Don't you think that would be a snapper for him?"

"I suppose he could. Of course, Albert has a big ego, I'm told. We're not the only ones with egos. Maybe his ego wouldn't permit him to turn out work like that."

"Perhaps," I said. "Well, I've got to walk. How much time do you need on the million?"

"Giiilll," he dragged it out in a special plea this time.

"Sorry, Franklin, I have no choice in the matter. Lot of pressures on me here. My heart is with you, but it's pocketbook time at *oy vay* corral."

"Gil!"

"Twenty-four hours," I said. "I'll call you."

I heard him wail as I hung up the phone.

18

The next morning, I awoke to the banging sounds of Jane Eaton coming through the door of her apartment. She was lugging three large canvases, which, on closer inspection, turned out to be the paintings I had purchased from Albert Durant, which he had unceremoniously switched on me.

Jane, I noticed through bleary eyes, looked different from when she left last night.

The clothes were the same, though they appeared to have been applied to her sensual body with less care. But the garish makeup had been wiped (or kissed) clean off. She looked a great deal more wholesome than when she left, but she also looked exhausted.

"What time is it?" I muttered, my eyes half-opened.

"Almost seven," she said cheerily. "Time to rise and shine."

I groaned and turned over.

"Hey, come on," she said, "up, up—we have work to do."

"Work?" I turned to face her. She was standing over my bed. "What work?"

"I got your paintings," she said, as if that answered the question.

"Have a good time at the hotel?" I asked.

She grinned. "I always have a good time when I'm working." She dropped down on the bed.

"Hey." I jerked away.

"Well, if you won't get up, I'll get down."

"I'm sleeping, for crying out loud."

"Poor baby," she said, caressing my brow with her fingertips.

"Hey!" I pushed her fingers off my brow—a real stupid thing to do.

"Oooo," she said, kissing her fingertips.

"Sorry," I said. "So where were you last night?"

"Working. You?"

"Working," I said, "and struggling to stay alive."

"Were you sick?"

"Someone tried to kill me."

"Kill you, Gil? What for?"

"Thought you might have an idea about that. I'm a blank."

"But I've no idea. Were you shot at or what?"

"A car tried to run me down."

She laughed. "Lot of crazy drivers in Zurich. I've had about a dozen close calls myself."

I shook my head. "This was no crazy driver. This was an assassin."

"Oh, Gilly pie," she said, tweaking my nose annoyingly, "who would want to kill such a sweetie pie?"

"I thought I'd ask *you* that question."

"*Me?*" She blanched. "I have no idea. It certainly wasn't me. And if I ever heard anyone simply propose such a thing, I'd bite off their earlobes."

"That's very reassuring," I said. "All I have to do now is scour Zurich for some fellas without earlobes." I turned my back to her.

"Now, Gil," she said, pawing my shoulder to indicate the direction she wished me to turn. "Look at me. I have good news for you."

"Good news?" I said, turning only my face to her. "What good news?"

"I found the Monet."

I not only turned the rest of my body toward where

Jane sat on the edge of my bed; her bed, actually, but I had been sleeping in it.

"You did?" I sat up. "Fantastic! Where?"

"Are you ready to talk business?"

My eyes were open to the room now. There was sunlight lighting the dust particles, and the room and the furnishings had a rosy pink-beige glow about them. Jane herself looked a little pinky in the early morning light filtering through the shutters. The whole thing added up to a calm about the place that almost put me back to sleep—if it weren't for Jane's news about having the Monet, and her enigmatic talk of business.

"May I see the Monet?" I said.

"Certainly," she said, but made no move.

"Where is it?"

"All in good time, Gil. Can we make a deal?"

"Deal?"

"You help me, I help you."

"Oh, that. That's a condition of showing me?"

"Your agreement to cooperate, yes," she said. "I'll show it to you after you agree to cooperate. You don't have to do anything more than agree. After you've seen it we'll get down to basics."

"How long will it take you to get it?"

"Get it?" she said. "I *have* it."

"*Here?* In this apartment?"

She nodded.

I started to get out of bed. She pushed me back down. "Just a minute," she said. "Agree?"

"I don't know what I'm agreeing to," I confessed, without my eagerness to see the Monet (and my million) dimming.

"The first thing you must understand before you go out on a limb is the 'Monet,' as you call it, is indubitably a fake."

"Well, what good would a fake do me?"

"I don't know, that's your decision."

"Well, I can tell you right now a copy of the picture

I'm after is worthless to me. You think I'd want to fool my principal even if he could be fooled?"

"You don't understand, silly boy," she said, tugging my ears this time. Those little endearments annoyed me. For the record anyway. Actually, between us, I rather liked the attention. "The painting you are looking for, I have found. You are looking for a fake. Monet never painted that painting you carry around with you—that picture is a picture of a fake. I have that fake. If it would do you any good to possess it temporarily, that is the arrangement I am offering you—in exchange for your evidence and sworn testimony."

"Sworn testimony?" I said. "My, my, it's getting heavier and heavier."

She watched me expectantly.

"You mean the thing has been here all this time?"

"No, I just got it."

My head swiveled around the room. She stopped my ridiculous motion with her two hands, one on each of my ears. Then she planted a huge, wet kiss on my lips, almost smothering me to death. But I gotta tell you this, if she had smothered me to death, I'd have died happy.

"Mmm," I mumbled when I came up for air, "that's very persuasive salesmanship."

"Good," she said, and smacked again my lips with hers.

"Okay," I said, "let's see the painting so we can attend to more important matters." Even as I said it, I hated myself for two-timing Sarah, that wonderful young woman. Thoughts of my wife floated in and out, but mostly out. I hated myself, but in a nice way.

"Not so fast," she said, "let's be clear on what I'm expecting. You must tell us everything you know about the incident."

"Who is us?"

"The police, of course. Interpol. Art-fraud division."

"You're sure this is an intentional art fraud?"

"We're sure," she said. "Of course, our case is not complete. Being sure and being in possession of enough evidence to convict can be kilometers apart. You are our ace."

"Me?" I marveled at my importance.

She nodded and watched my expression.

"But what about my fee?"

"Fee? We don't pay," she said. "Oh, I might finagle minimal expenses on the thing."

"I'm talking about my fee from my principal."

"Oh, that," she said. "I'm afraid that's out of our hands. I don't mind cooperating with you if there is something we can do to help on that score."

"It's a contingency fee. No painting, no fee."

"Of course," she said. "I understand."

"Would you be prepared to let me have the painting to deliver it to my principal so I could bank my fee before I have to render assistance in your...prosecution?"

"I think we could work that out."

"Deal," I said, beaming, and she kissed me again.

19

Of course, I stipulated with Jane that after she showed me the painting I would have twelve hours to change my mind. If d'Lacy had managed to put the million in escrow, I would feel less salubrious about selling him down the river.

I still thought he could be an innocent in this con, but my doubts were growing.

"Okay," I said, "let's see the painting."

She stood up.

"I can't believe you have it here. I'd certainly have seen it. Did you come in before I saw you? In the middle of the night maybe?"

"I was working, remember?"

If she wanted to perpetuate the fiction that she was a hooker, I wasn't going to make a case against. Maybe that was her relationship to Durant. Sarah saying it was an on-again, off-again thing didn't gainsay that.

Jane moved to the living room. I loved to watch her move. In a moment she was back with one of the paintings I had chosen from Albert Durant's *oeuvre*. She turned it to face toward me. It was the nighttime scene with the lights that reminded me of the Monet London thing.

"Here it is," she said, holding it in front of her chest and therefore blocking the best view.

"Here's what?" I asked, confused.

"Your painting."

"That's one I bought from Durant, yes."

"You didn't know what you were getting," she said.

"I don't get it."

"You don't see it?" she said. "Here, you take the painting and stare at it. I think you'll be surprised at what you see." She handed me the painting—flopped it on my lap in bed is what she really did.

Jane never went anywhere in the apartment that my eyes left her, so rather than stare at the painting I stared at her. When she disappeared out of sight I looked back at the painting. I liked it, that's why I bought it—besides trying to ingratiate myself with the forger by showing an appreciation for his original art, which no one would buy.

Whoops! Eyes up. Jane came back into the room carrying a bowl of water and a sponge. "See anything yet?" she asked.

I shook my head.

"Here," she said, gliding across the bedroom floor to sit back down next to me on the bed again. The bowl was balanced between her thighs. I held the painting while she wet the sponge and dabbed it on the canvas near the bottom-right corner. With a gentle, circular motion the dark color gave way to the gray beneath. Soon the signature was revealed:
MONET

"Sacred smoke," I said, as she kept rubbing to reveal the Monet underneath. It was the real thing all right.

"Now you see why Durant switched them on you?"

I nodded, though my first thought, unspoken, was that I had bought the painting and it was, ergo, rightfully mine.

"But who made the original switch?" I asked.

Jane stared at me.

"Don't you know?" I prodded her.

"Of course I know," she said. "What I don't know is why you want to know."

"Just wondered. No reason really. It's all a bit confusing."

"A bit," she agreed.

"Shall we take the sponge to my other two Durants?" I asked.

"I don't think you'll get the same result."

"Why not? He switched all three, didn't he?"

"Sure, he didn't want to make you suspicious," she said. "But you're welcome to try the sponge."

"No, thanks," I said, "I like them the way they are."

"Albert will give you another painting of your choice," Jane said, "or your money back on this one—as you prefer."

"No," I said, "I'm satisfied with what I bought."

"Well, I suppose he'd be glad to paint you another just like this looked."

I shook my head. "No, I like this just as it is."

"Oh, pooh," she said and disappeared into the bathroom for her shower. She didn't close the door so, naturally, I watched the whole thing. These last days, since I landed in London, had been a wild dream. How a dull vanilla guy like me could land face up in this wonderland I didn't even want to contemplate for fear it would all evaporate.

She fled the shower and dried herself, making no attempt to hide her special charms from old Vanilla. In her heyday old Tyranny Rex never looked anything like that.

Jane threw on her clothes faster than any kid late for school.

She was the antithesis of the professional the night before. Her dress was demure, her hair was in a bun and her face untarnished by makeup.

"You're going to contact your principal so we can talk."

"I should have my answer by five," I said, but she was already out the door. I didn't tell her that million bucks from Franklin d'Lacy did just not seem in the checkers.

One thing was certain. If her proposition included her, it would be almost impossible to resist. Like someone making an offer you can't refute.

When the door closed behind my policewoman,

hooker or just plain Jane, I dropped back on the bed and considered my options. The only way I could see d'Lacy getting the million before he got the picture was from Michael Hadaad. Then I considered the odds of that happening and decided they were laughable. I could not conceive of any reason Hadaad would want me to succeed. Not if it meant earning a fee. *Never* if it meant getting another penny from him.

Why he recommended me to d'Lacy in the first place continued to nag at me. d'Lacy insisted repeatedly Hadaad was a friend. As such, I would have to believe he wanted d'Lacy, and therefore me, to succeed.

But could he want d'Lacy to succeed and me to fail? More likely. But how to bring that about is less obvious. But maybe not. If d'Lacy got the picture and I didn't get the fee, Hadaad would be happy. But how could they get me to do that? With all I put Hadaad through to get my fee on his case, how could he assume I'd roll over and play deceased on this one?

I realized I'd achieved what I thought would be the hardest part of the case: I found the painting. Now, other factors were cropping up; factors which seemed even more insurmountable than finding the painting.

One, Jane says it's a fake. Just like that! She reverses the opinion of one of the leading museum directors in the world. I would discount what she said, but she is a police expert on art fraud. Or so I have been led to believe.

Second dilemma: If it is a fraud, could d'Lacy really have been fooled, or is their game a different kettle of crabs? And if it is, what is it? A simple scam for money? It just seems unlikely.

The third question is the biggest. How do I parlay all these impossible factors into my million-dollar fee? If the thing *is* a fake, why would anyone pay me anything for it? Is there some other reason I should schlepp halfway across the world with that picture?

But the picture was still here. Did she trust me, or didn't she care?

I would have to make some foolproof plan of escape. It would be nice if Jane went back to Albert Durant's tonight, I thought.

I heard the sound of the mailman on the stairs. A moment later he shoved a fistful of envelopes and magazines through the mail slot. Out of curiosity I rifled through the stuff—commercial messages, a few bills, and then I saw it—an overnight letter addressed to me with Sarah's return address in London.

I tore open the envelope to feel first, then see a couple Polaroid pictures taken outside the Jacques Moran Gallery. They were pictures of a darkish-skinned man, unknown to me at first. Then I realized who they were.

Both were pictures of Michael Hadaad.

20

The famous picture was still here—in Jane's living room. Some folks paid sixteen million for the opus, and here it was, sitting in broad daytime as though it had been picked up at JCPenney.

That was a real testimony to Jane's belief that it was a forgery, I thought.

But even if it was, was it a *worthless* forgery, or would I get a million for delivering it as agreed?

Was there any reason I couldn't walk out of there now with my three paintings? I had paid for them in hard-earned coin of the realm, had I not? Ergo, they were MINE! Now I had the sinking feeling that Jane would not genuflect to that point of view, but what the heck, did she leave me alone with the legendary painting, or what?

So why not, I thought, put it to the test? Take my paintings out of the apartment and see if the sky fell on me in the form of Interpol or some other worthies.

Next I had to decide if I wanted to hide them. Take them off the frames, roll them up—but that wouldn't be a true test. Let's have them in the open. I could say, if stopped, I bought them. If a fuss was made about the "Monet," I would say I was taking it to an art house for another opinion. Not a bad idea anyway.

So I gathered up the paintings, and my meager belongings which I had brought for the trip, and went out the door. I didn't leave Jane a note because I fully expected to be back.

I trod lightly at first, scrutinizing every face I saw along the way—staying far to the inside of the sidewalks until I could flag a taxi. I watched every car and every driver for signs they might be watching, pursuing or just following me.

When I finally got into a cab, I thought I could taste victory. "Green Hotel," I said, directing him to an out-of-the-way, unpopular, down-at-heel sort of place, where I didn't expect to be run down by a car or even located.

With the paintings and my overnight bag at my feet, I checked into the Green Hotel. I'm not sure why they called it the *Green* Hotel. It wasn't green and it wasn't on Green Street. Perhaps it was for the solo, dusty potted palm in—if I may speak in hyperbole—the lobby (a *Howea forsteriana,* a.k.a. the Kentia palm). On further reflection, I think it was for the U.S. greenbacks they socked into the till with their outrageous prices. The clerk was a made-up woman who must have been younger than she looked. Her hair was bottleblond and her mouth seemed undergirded with elastic, for every time she was about to speak, the elastic tightened.

"A room with a telephone," I asked for. "Economy," I added.

And economy it was. It faced another window, and was so close, if anyone sneezed in one room, the other would get the chicken pox.

I can't say the Swiss have a misunderstanding of the word "economy." Except that for the price of the room, I could have gotten a suite in the U.S. This was economy like the real McGillah. There was a bed and a telephone—I hadn't bothered to mention a bath, so there wasn't one. Old Purse Mouth sure showed me.

I stowed the pictures under the bed. I wasn't being devious, there just wasn't any other place for them.

Then I reached for the phone. Notice I didn't say "went for the phone." There was no need for that drastic an action. You could reach the phone from anywhere in the room.

It was a little after seven a.m. Los Angeles time, and again I decided to put d'Lacy's word to the test. Was he always at his desk by seven?

I rang him up, as we say over here.

He didn't answer. After ten rings or so I had another idea. I rang up the Grand Hotel.

"Jacques Moran, por favor."

I didn't expect him to be in at four-fifteen in the afternoon, but he was. He seemed a little groggy when he answered.

"Mr. Moran?"

"Yessss?"

"This is Gil Yates. Remember, I spoke with you in your room yesterday?"

"I remember," he said, I thought a little shortly.

"Did I wake you?"

"Yes."

"Sorry, shall I call back?"

"Depends, what's it about?"

"I have the painting."

"You have the what? Not the Monet?"

"Yes. What would you give for it?"

"Everything I have," he said. "If you really have the Monet."

"Some people think it's a fake."

"There was a fake—which do you have?"

"I have the one you packed in the crate."

"All right, what do you want for it?"

"A million," I said. When he didn't gasp, I added, "American dollars."

"Done," he said.

I swallowed. Hard. "When can you have it?" I asked.

"When do you want it?"

"This afternoon?"

"Realistically. I could probably have it tomorrow by around noon."

"Sounds good."

"I'd have to see the painting first," he said, "before I

arranged for the money."

"Fair enough. I will call you back when I have a definite answer from my principal."

"d'Lacy," Moran murmured.

I didn't argue. "We'll arrange a meeting place."

"What's the matter with here at my hotel?"

"Oh, not much. Only that when I left you someone tried to run me down in the street with a car."

"Well, it wasn't me."

"I'd just rather not give whoever it was another shot."

"All right, name your place."

"I'll get back to you," I said, and hung up.

Then I dialed Franklin d'Lacy in Los Angeles again. I don't know why; I knew he didn't have the money and Moran was eager to give it to me. It would have been so much simpler. Same town, no hassle. But I felt I had an obligation to the guy who hired me. That's just the kind of guy I am: steady, loyal, reliable—law-abiding. In all my life I can't ever remember leaving my house without taking my driver's license with me. Even if I wasn't driving.

d'Lacy picked up the phone on the first ring.

"Hi," I said nonchalantly.

"Gil!" he said. "You have it?"

"I have it."

He was stunned to silence. Did the great museum director misunderstand what I said? "You have the money?"

"In escrow. A cool million. You'll be rich."

"Where did you get it?"

"Do you care? If I got it from the tooth fairy, would you turn it down?"

"I guess not."

"You drive a hard bargain, but I'm serious about it so I've escrowed the money. Just need your signature on a couple papers. They'll take a fax for now. Shall I fax to the London number?"

"What? Oh, yes, that will be fine," I said. Then I complicated matters which were already too complicated.

"People here say it's a forgery."

"Then they're looking at a different painting," he said. "I'm not paying for a forgery, of course. I hope that's understood."

"Well, yes and no. If I bring the picture you photographed, I expect my fee."

"Certainly."

"Even if it is later proven a forgery?"

"You sure you have the same painting? The Monet?"

"The Monet as in your picture."

"So who says that's a forgery?"

"Well, a lot of people who seem to know what they're talking about."

"Well, they don't know what they're talking about."

"Oh, by the way," I said, "did you know Hadaad was in London?"

"Yes. He's trying to get some leads on the painting."

"Doesn't trust me, after recommending me?"

"Now, Gil. We're beside ourselves. Our trusted dealer has disappeared."

"But I found him. I told you that."

"Yes, but remember, you wouldn't tell me where he *or* you were."

"Does it matter?"

"To us. Put yourself in our place if you can."

"How about putting yourself in my place. Someone tried to kill me when I left Moran."

"Where was that?"

"In front of his hotel."

"Which hotel?"

Oh, my, I thought, he must think I'm asleep. "Is that important? If it were the tooth fairy's hangout, would that tell you anything?"

"Okay, Gil, we're on the same side, remember? Just get me the picture A.S.A.P. My hide is already in the soup here."

"I had an idea, Mr. d'Lacy. To expedite things."

"What kind of idea?"

"You and Moran are on the same side in this thing, aren't you?"

"Well, we were."

"I mean, you both want the painting restored to you to save your reputations."

"I suppose that's true," he said in the phone, "but ever since he disappeared without a word to us we've been on pins and needles. I'm convinced the switch was made at his end and he was responsible for it."

"Do you think he did it himself?"

"I didn't—but the law allows flight to be considered a confirmation of guilt. So I don't know. Why all these questions about Moran?"

"You do know he doesn't have the painting. I have it. If he had switched the painting himself, why wouldn't he still have it?"

"I hope you're right. I'm betting a mil on you."

"That's my question. Moran is obligated to deliver this painting to you?"

"Yes, he is."

"So why don't we work it through him?"

"How's that?"

"He's agreed to give me the million by noon tomorrow. Seems to me he is the one should pay. Save you a million—make a quick, easy transfer here. What do you say?"

"Absolutely not!"

21

The guy who never leaves home without his driver's license, the guy who has worked for his father-in-law for twenty-some straight years and the guy who has been faithfully married to the same domineering wife for precisely the same amount of time is in a quandary. Well, "faithfully" is a matter of interpretation, I guess. In the strictest sense we could say "faithfully until now."

Confucius say a million in hand is worth more in the bush. I was walking distance from one million, and nine time zones from the other. I had to consider the logistics of the thing. What kind of difficulty would I have getting a sixteen-million-dollar painting through customs? Wouldn't it be *some*thing if I could get the million from each of them? *Two* million. I didn't want to be greedy, but I didn't want to miss a perfectly good opportunity either.

I thought of taking the Monet back to Albert Durant for another coat of the water paint, but decided I'd never get it back.

I had told d'Lacy to fax immediately the escrow instructions to Sarah's gallery. If he'd really done it, I was committed.

I called Sarah. She had the fax. I made arrangements with the hotel to receive it and called her back with the number. A few minutes later I could hear the grinding sound of the fax machine receiving the goods.

The desk clerk handed me the fax and I handed him

twenty Swiss francs for his trouble. I stood at the counter, reading the escrow instructions. The company was a place called Alpine Escrow, which struck me as a strange name for a Los Angeles flatland escrow. But underneath, it said, "Lou Alpine, President." There was no address or phone on the form, but the fax number was typed in.

The language of the instructions was clear enough. It stated that Monet Art Incorporated, a California corporation, had deposited one million dollars in escrow to be paid to Gil Yates under the following conditions:

1. Upon delivery by Gil Yates to Franklin d'Lacy, LAMMA, a certain painting known as Flag Street, an oil by Monet.

2. With the acceptance and physical possession of said Monet painting by Mr. d'Lacy, the escrow funds shall be irrevocably paid to Mr. Yates.

3. If acceptance by Mr. d'Lacy is not made, Mr. Yates may retain possession of said Monet painting and escrow funds shall be released to Monet Art Incorporated with no further liability on their part to Gil Yates, his successors or assigns.

With the Alpine papers were the signed authorization accepting Moran's authorization for the Monet. Later I faxed back all that was required of me.

I could see the fine hand of Hadaad and his lawyers on the documents. It seemed I could hardly lose. If I delivered the right painting, they wanted it. If it was wrong, they would back up that judgment by allowing me to keep it.

But then what? How easy to hit me over the head and steal it. How simple to claim it was an artful forgery. Then, after stealing it from me, they just claim it is the original. I could, and would, sign the edge of the canvas in back, but that could easily be cut off. I would sign in thin indelible pen behind the darkest portion. But if they cared enough, they could easily dispose of me. Gil Yates, in my configuration anyway, doesn't exist—who'd miss me? Malvin Stark would be listed as missing in Europe—disappeared without a trace. That was one of the dangers of this anonymous business and keeping it from my family.

But of the two, I had more faith in Jacques Moran than in Franklin d'Lacy. I thought I had a fairer shot at the money, this escrow notwithstanding.

I called Moran back. He answered eagerly.

"Bad news," I said.

"Oh," his voice sank to a basso register I didn't realize he was capable of.

"My principal claims to have raised my fee, so I am obligated to him."

"Oh."

"I should think that okay with you, since you only want to get the painting back to him."

"Yes, but my reputation has been damaged. I am being held responsible for this, ah, mishap. I would much prefer to shepherd the Monet back to d'Lacy myself."

"That's worth a million to you?"

"Certainly. What price can you put on your reputation?"

I've thought of selling mine for a couple hundred sometimes, but I didn't tell him. A lot of people would consider my reputation, at a couple hundred, overpriced.

"You have that much lying around?" I asked.

"I told you I'd get it. I just made a very large sale, you'll remember."

"I wonder, before I go any further with ·this, would you be good enough to look at the painting and give me your opinion of its authenticity?"

"I'd be happy to."

He wanted to meet in his hotel room; I suggested a more neutral rendezvous. Not only because I was still smarting from my near-death experience, but also because I was unprotected and thought Moran might try to take the painting from me.

We agreed to meet at a café across the street from the Green Hotel, where I had rented a room for the day.

I watched from the lobby front window as Jacques Moran got out of his cab and dragged himself into the café.

He did not yet look as happy as I expected he would, considering he knew I had the missing painting.

I checked the streets for signs of another car that might have followed him. When I was satisfied I could cross the street without being murdered, I made my way carefully to the sidewalk. Then, making doubly sure there wasn't another kamikaze after me, I ran across the street and into the café, where Jacques Moran was waiting for me.

We shook hands. He looked frazzled, like a man spiritually exhausted. It was then I noticed he was wearing a blue blazer.

We found a table and he ordered strong coffee. I had hot chocolate.

"Ah, Jacques," I said.

"Where's the painting?"

"I notice you are wearing the blue blazer."

"You like it?"

"Love it. But you told me you didn't own a blue blazer—I went through your closet, remember?"

"It was at the cleaners." He shrugged. "People will lie to you when they are trying to save their skins."

"But I telephoned the cleaners..."

"In the hotel," he said. "You don't think I'd pay those prices..."

"But your hair was darker."

"Vegetable dye," he shrugged.

"But, why?"

"So I was out at Durant's. I was pretty sure he had the painting, but I turned the place upside down and didn't find it."

"What made you think he had it?"

"A hunch. Who else *could* have it?" He frowned. "Where's the painting?" he repeated.

"Close by," I said. "I wanted to make certain you were alone and I wouldn't be run down by another killer car."

"I had nothing to do with that," he said.

"I believe that," I said. "Until I start to think about it."

"What do you mean?"

"Who else knew I was at the Grand Hotel then?"

"I've no idea. Maybe someone followed you."

"Maybe," I said, not convinced.

"You don't think I could have picked up the phone and secured an assassin outside the hotel, given him your description and bam! he connects in just those few moments." He shook his head and waved his arm at the remoteness of the situation.

"A car phone?"

"You mean to say I have a man standing by outside my hotel twenty-four hours, just in case I feel like running someone down?"

"Okay," I said, "maybe it's pretty silly. But a lot of this caper seems to be pretty silly."

"Perhaps silliest of all is my meeting with you to see the painting, and you don't even *have* the painting."

"I have it."

"Then let's see it."

"A few questions first."

"Why?"

"I must decide to sell it to you, or to sell it to Franklin d'Lacy. You can help," I said. "Or how about Michael Hadaad?"

"Snake," he hissed.

"I couldn't agree with you more. But he might offer me more for the work than you and d'Lacy."

"Oh, I don't doubt he'd offer it. I just doubt you'd ever collect."

"Yes, I think I know that from bitter experience. Can you tell me where Hadaad is now?"

"No." His shudder told me that did not make him unhappy.

"How well do you know Michael Hadaad?"

"Too well."

"I gather he is not one of your favorite people."

"You gather correctly."

"Mine either." To break the snowballs, I told Moran

the story of how I did this big job for Hadaad, saving him twenty million dollars, and how he tried, with a gun, to renege.

"That's Hadaad," he said, sadly nursing his coffee.

"How is your gallery connected to him?"

His head jerked like it was going to roll off his shoulders.

"He seems to be there, now," I said, and pulled out the Polaroids to show him.

"He's tried to muscle into my business for several years. He came in as a customer some years ago—bought some expensive pieces—ingratiated himself. Told me he was on the LAMMA board and a confidant of the renowned Franklin d'Lacy and, as such, in a position to throw some nice business my way. All he wanted at first was knockdown prices. Later he wanted 'a piece of the action,' was the way I believe he put it." With his hand, Jacques Moran wiped away the disgust on his mouth. Out of mouth, out of mind.

"Did you give it to him?"

He shook his head, then sighed. "I held off as long as I could. The art market, which was swimming along so beautifully, suddenly sank. I had overextended. Things were going so well. Then, boom, I was about to lose my shop, and Sir Galahad steps in."

"Hadaad?"

"He doesn't want much: fifty-one-percent ownership, his prune-faced cousin to keep the books."

"In exchange for what?"

"A two-million-pound loan."

I whistled, not as softly as I had intended.

"I can buy the business back anytime I can pay back the loan with ten percent interest per annum. Of course, with him taking fifty-one percent of the profits and the art market blasted to hell, that is a very tough go."

"What was your profit on the Monet?"

"Two million pounds, about."

"So there you are."

He shook his head. "Hadaad has half that, remember."

I did.

"But it got me closer. Or would have." He looked me in the eye. "You *do* have it?"

"Yes. But how could you give me a million dollars?"

"Half from Hadaad. Of course, I might ask for a receipt for *two* million." Was this desperate guy actually winking at me or were his contact lenses kicking up?

"Do you think Hadaad could have been involved in the switch?"

He looked at me as though I had just demonstrated an infallible metaphysical perception. "I'm sure he is."

"Why?"

"To break me."

"How so?"

"I make this great discovery. It is almost enough to get me in the clearing. He doesn't want that. Hadaad brooks no challenges to his absolute power. To him I am just a worm to be crushed."

"But if he was in on the switch, why do *I* have the painting?"

"That is yet to be proven, of course; but assuming you do, and you may well have because obviously he doesn't have it, something must have gone wrong."

"How could anyone crack the security of that trucking company?"

"Not easily. But look at the Brinks robbery some years back. Nothing is impossible—especially when you have at your command Hadaad's ill-gotten means."

"What about d'Lacy?" I asked him. "How does he fit here?"

"Another dupe of Hadaad's." He winced. "Perhaps that's a little strong. Hadaad's a criminal, you know. Been to jail."

I nodded.

"Fellas like that are usually pariahs, especially in the up-market snob realm of art-museum boards. Hadaad was willing to dump tons of money on d'Lacy; all he had to do was legitimize this gunrunner by putting him on the board.

There was, of course, the expected hue and cry, but d'Lacy and ten million dollars made in astute brokerage of instruments of death, much of them used against your own country, ruled the day."

"Now they're pals?"

"I wouldn't go that far. d'Lacy isn't Pollyanna. He tolerates him in exchange for his undying support on the board, where d'Lacy needs every friend he can get."

"How do you rate d'Lacy's art savvy?"

"Top drawer."

"He swears this Monet is an original."

"So do I."

"Yet I am told again and again it is a forgery."

"Let me see it," he said, spreading his hands.

I paid the bill, and took Moran across the street to the plain hotel that almost disappeared in the surrounding buildings. We walked up the steps to my room. I had taken care to see we were not followed.

I let us in the room with the old-fashioned keyhole-lock key and asked him to sit on the bed, while I pulled the three paintings from under it.

Carefully I laid the "Monet" on the bed.

Jacques Moran barely looked at it. "That's it!" he cried.

22

Jacques Moran begged me to sell him the painting. He would take it to d'Lacy or Hadaad and double his money, buy his way out from under Hadaad.

I told him his offer was tempting, but I made an agreement to return the work to d'Lacy in Los Angeles and I was a guy, I said, who honored my commitments.

"I'd be happy to have you go along," I said, and he gladly accepted the offer.

From my vantage point—telling this tale—I can see that I should have wondered why he didn't just call the police, tell them I had in my possession a stolen painting, and take it back—without paying me a nickel.

I kidded myself that he liked me and wanted me to earn a fee, so long as the picture got back to d'Lacy and Moran would no longer be suspected of cheating LAMMA.

I also believed that he was willing to give a million because he could get more from the insurance company. Though I don't understand how that works. I guess he would sell it to the insurance company through a third party for a couple million or so. The company, ostensibly, getting a great deal–saving paying off sixteen million. d'Lacy had mentioned it. I suppose everybody in the art game knows all the angles. Didn't seem too ethical to me—but, then, I was, as they say, a babe in the forest.

We got in a taxi with my overnight bag and the paintings—we drove first to his hotel, where I waited in the taxi for him to pack and check out.

I thought of calling Jane to say goodbye and thanks, then realized how absolutely stupid that would be.

What a conundrum this was. Jane has in her possession a painting sold for sixteen million bucks—just sitting there in her living room while d'Lacy, Moran and Hadaad are salivating to get it back. I guess since she thought it was a fake, it wasn't worth very much. But why not keep it at Interpol as evidence of the forgery? Why bring it to me at all?

Coming to think of it, I really didn't have any hard evidence Jane worked for Interpol. Oh, she gave me a card, all right, but those are a cinch to make in the computer age. Her Interpol could even be a dress shop.

Jacques Moran came flying out the door. While he was packing he had the concierge check the flights to Los Angeles. We could get one in a little less than an hour if we hurried.

The cab driver stepped on it. He drove so fast and recklessly that I decided *he* could have been the guy who almost hit me. On reflection, I decided he was trying to please an American who might ignore the sign on the meter that said the tip was included in the fare. Of course, to collect a tip he would have to deliver his passengers alive, and the way he was going that was a very long shot.

The picturesque Swiss countryside blurred past as we sped to our escape. The way I looked at it, if I survived the reckless speeding to the airport, I had a pretty good lock on the million. If d'Lacy weaseled out, Jacques Moran stood ready to pay it.

The way I saw it, both fellas seemed ready, willing and suitable to bilk the insurance company. If it got me a million, the way I saw it, I was in the clear, ethically. Of course, we believe what we want to believe. I just knew I didn't want to mess with an insurance company—not for ten times the amount.

I wondered how that bargaining worked. It must have been something like a kidnapping ransom. The thief wanted as much as he could get, and the insurance company wanted the stolen goods for as big a discount as they could get.

I didn't steal the picture, I bought it. Of course, I had knowledge it was stolen, which may have forestalled any aspirations I entertained of being mistaken for Saint Augustine. What I still didn't understand was who stole it, and why. And how it wound up back with the guy who Jane says forged it.

Of course, the guy sitting beside me in the rocket-powered taxi swore it was genuine. He had a lot more experience in these matters than Jane had. My sympathies were with him because I had a lot better chance at my million smugolies if the Monet were the real McKay.

Miracle of miracles, our driver pulled up to the curb in front of Swissair and my heart was still beating: rather wildly, as I recall. Jacques hopped out of the cab before the driver would have a chance to take off again, and coincidentally leaving me to pay the fare.

Following Jacques' lead, I too escaped the rocket chamber to the relative safety of the sidewalk with my bag and the three paintings. As I reached for my wallet I considered the dilemma of the tip. Pro: He did get us here fast. We had a good thirty minutes to plane time—and he got us here alive, if slightly deranged. Con: Madmen should not be encouraged. Someday, if I encourage him with my tip, he's liable to kill someone. Then I would have that on my conscience. Then there was the sign in the cab about the tip already being in the fare, like the tips are on the restaurant checks. It's a rather nice feature of Europe, that. Who am I to upset the apple wagon, to subvert the system? Pro again: I expect this driver, who has just this minute completed his pilot training, would be disappointed not to be rewarded for his heroism. Besides, I was sure he wouldn't like me.

So I slipped him an extra fiver. A guy who was about to land himself a cool million could do no less. After he thanked me and pulled away from the curb, I tried to analyze the thank you. Was it sincere? Effusive enough? Did he expect more? Should I have given him more? Did he think I was a patsy to give him anything extra?

Jacques and I lugged our stuff to the counter, where an austere young woman with *sehr gute* English greeted us with official efficiency, as she had several hundred others every day. The Swiss have a mania for fairness (or neutrality: See World War II) and it wouldn't be seemly to heap more warmth on one party than the other. So their solution was to save that warmth—perhaps for World War III.

Jacques went first. I was happy his spirits had picked up considerably. Perhaps because he expected to lose his life in a taxi crash he now had a new rent on life. Jacques was more ebullient than I'd ever seen him. His chin was up, there was a sparkle in his eye, and he even told this mud fence she was an attractive woman. She thanked him without looking up, as though he had offered her a suggestion for relief from bunions.

Jacques, ticketed for the flight and ready to go, moved aside for me to face the woman who uncannily reminded me of my wife in her prime. If she had a prime. I couldn't remember. I handed over my passport and credit card, and said I'd like a couple seats on the flight to Los Angeles.

"Two?" she asked.

"Yes. One for me, one for my special painting."

She looked at my stuff that I had shoved onto the scale under the counter. "You have two paintings here. They aren't wrapped. I'm afraid we can't take them like that."

"Can you wrap them for me?"

"Oh, I can't do that. We couldn't be responsible."

"Do you have something I can wrap them in?"

She looked at me and I saw what little patience she had drain from her impersonal face. "No."

"All right, I'll carry all of them—put them in the extra seat I'm buying." That may have satisfied her. If it caused any happiness in that Alpine heart of hers, I didn't detect it.

She turned to my passport and started pounding her

computer. She peered at the screen, then pounded some more. Then again. I was watching the clock. Fifteen minutes to flight time, not too bad, I thought.

Finally she looked up and said, "I'm having trouble finding two seats together. Could you wait here a minute? I'll be right back—"

She picked up my passport and disappeared through the door behind her to that nether world to which all airline-counter employees repair, sooner or later. It was an inner sanctum where I imagined all the sexual harassment took place.

After she was gone five minutes I started to fidget. I told Jacques he ought to go to the gate. I guess he suspected I was trying to shake him, because he shook his head and said, "I'm not going without you and the Monet. What would be the point?" He looked down at the Monet at my feet. "You know, the general public's ignorance of art notwithstanding, you really should cover that up. I'd feel a lot safer."

"Think someone's liable to recognize it and hit me over the head for it?"

"A lot stranger things have happened."

"Want to see if the shop has any paper they'll sell us?"

"Okay." He started to move. Then stopped. "We'll do it on the way to the plane."

Not this plane. Our young ticketing agent came back with the news that she couldn't get me on this plane with the painting. The computer had garbled the information and there were no seats left. But they had another flight in two hours that went to New York, then on to Los Angeles. "Would you like me to book you on that flight?"

I shrugged my shoulders. "Unless there's something else earlier? Another airline?"

"There isn't," she said.

Jacques stepped up to the counter. "I'll change mine too," he said.

She looked at him as though that were a strange

idea. Then said, in one of those voices that indicate the opposite, "All right."

She issued our tickets and gave us a handwritten note. "Swissair apologizes for your inconvenience. We'd like you to be our guest in the first-class lounge while you are waiting." Then she gave us directions.

Jacques was delighted with that accommodation and so was I.

We stopped by the shop and bought enough wrapping paper and tape to cover the Monet on the paint side. Then we made our way to the first-class lounge. The girl at the door was more adroit at smiling, and when she asked to see our tickets I gave her the note.

"Oh, good," she said, "make yourself at home. The bar is to the right. You may help yourself to the hors d'oeuvre, and if you need anything, don't hesitate to ask."

Jacques and I moved into the lounge and spread out on the generous leather seats. He ordered a Bloody Mary; I had an orange juice.

"This is more like it," he said as we settled back in our chairs with our drinks and a little plate of munchies each.

Then I realized how lucky I was that no one called me "Mr. Stark" while Jacques was around, saving me untold embarrassing explanations. He knew me only as Gil Yates.

The first-class lounge had newspapers from all over the world. I picked up the *Los Angeles Times* and searched for news of Franklin d'Lacy. I was methodically reading the paper from front to back when I saw them enter the lounge. I looked for another exit—there was none.

"Uh-oh," I said sotto voce to Jacques. "You don't know me."

He looked up from his magazine. I buried my head in the newspaper. Some effective hiding place, with the "Monet" at my feet.

Jane came toward me with two hulking bruisers in suits on either side of her, one making no attempt to hide the handcuffs dangling from his belt.

23

"Well, Gil," Jane said, always super-cheerful. Then she dropped her voice to a stage whisper. "Or should I say Malvin?" She waited for an answer.

"You decide," I muttered.

"I see you've brought a painting or two with you."

"Yes, I bought three from Albert Durant, remember?" There it was. I'd just trotted out my meager defense.

"Well...yes," she said, and laughed so I thought the whole place would shake. I could feel Jacques turning blue beside me, but he kept his face to his magazine as though he didn't know me. "To think," she said, catching her breath, "you must have thought I was a fake—or a poser, and would just let you slip out of the country. Why, Malvin, you didn't even say goodbye. No note. No nothing."

"Sorry," I whimpered. "I had only planned to take the painting for another opinion."

"Did you get it?"

"Yes. A real Monet."

"Wonderful. All the more reason for you to slip to the States with it on the seat beside you. Of course, I noticed you had the foresight to take all your things with you while you were having the little darling appraised."

I shrugged my shoulders and blushed. There was no question of making a run for it through the two Matterhorns she'd brought along. Frankly, I wouldn't give much for my chances of outrunning Jane alone. So the ball was in her alley, as they say.

"Well," she said, still smiling, "I am glad I caught you in time for a proper goodbye. So why don't we all go down to the station and have a little chat?"

"And then I can go?"

"Oh, I expect you can," she said, "sooner or later. What do you say boys?" she asked the mountains. Together they gave what seemed to be a single "I don't know" gesture. Whatever they were trying to convey, it did not fill me with optimism.

Jane was talking again. "Al, why don't you give Malvin a hand with his paintings. Hans, take his bag."

"I can carry it," I said too quickly.

"Nonsense," Jane said. "Any man who flies first-class doesn't need to carry his own bags." The boys picked up my stuff. "Now, how do you feel about handcuffs?" she asked me. "Would it make you at all self-conscious if we slipped them on you? You could cover them with a coat or something."

"I'd rather not," I acknowledged. "Don't worry," I said, gesturing by flipping my head between the two mountains, "I won't run."

Jane had another good laugh. She was in awfully good spirits. "What do you say, boys? Al? Hans?"

One of them grunted the consensus in Swiss-German. I assumed it freely translated to "This wimp isn't going nowhere."

Jane giggled. "Okay, Malvin, you're on your honor. Now this is what you get for hurting my feelings by not saying goodbye."

I wondered if she meant to make me feel like an errant child being scolded by a stern mom.

I noticed Jacques Moran had sunk further down in the seat, and his concentration on his magazine was so intense he was perspiring profusely, causing little rivers of sweat to run in the furrows of his brow.

As the boys led me out, Jane, in what seemed like an afterthought but certainly wasn't, turned to Jacques and said, "Almost, Moran, but no cigar. Stay local. Call me tomorrow around nine, will you, please?" She handed him a card, which he took without closing his mouth. "If you decide not to return to the Grand Hotel, please let us know where you're staying." She said it as though she were a Southern hostess, knocking herself out to please.

"But I have a ticket..." he started to protest.

"Canceled," she said. "But refundable," she added, reassuringly, winking broadly and devastatingly at him as she joined us for our ignominious exit.

She walked ahead with me. The enforcers were behind, carrying my stuff. "Really, Gil," she said, "what *could* you have been thinking? Wait!" She put up her hand. "Don't tell me. You believed the bit about me being a hooker, but not about being a cop."

"I don't know," I mumbled. "You didn't seem too concerned. I mean, you left me right there with the painting. I mean, I thought you thought it was a forgery, and I didn't know if you were right, so I guess I thought it was worthless to you—but worth a lot to...somebody."

"To *you*, you mean?" she said. "Well, it is worthless as a painting, of course. But, not worthless as evidence. I'm just so disappointed we have to go through this whole charade—good as I've been to you." She gave me a little affectionate bump with her elbow.

"You don't have to go through any of this for me," I assured her.

She looked over at me and smiled that bedroom smile of hers. Then she rubbed the back of my neck and all my blood rushed there while I kissed her hand. "I appreciate that, Gil," she said. "I really do."

And it didn't even sound like she was mocking me, but of course she was.

Their car, unmarked, was still at the curb. No one had ticketed it.

She got in the back with me. The Alps got in front. Hans looked back. "Sure you don't want to cuff him, Lieutenant?"

"Oh, my Malvin's safe with me—aren't you, Malvin?"

Answering a question with a question, I asked, "How do you know my name is Malvin?"

"Your passport, silly."

"I never showed you my passport," I said, and immediately realized how silly that was.

She dropped a hand on my thigh and squeezed it, followed by a conspiratorial wink.

"So what's in store for me?" I asked. "Whatever my name is."

She laughed. "It's good to keep your sense of humor, Mal," she said. "Anybody ever call you Mal?"

I shook my head.

"Nothing wrong with it," she said. "So what's in store, you want to know? Well, we're going to headquarters for a chat. I expect there will be a little good cop, bad cop routine—to scare the wits out of you, you know, then love you up and display the rosy scenario if you cooperate."

"You going to lock me up?"

"Oh, we'll make you comfy, Mal, don't worry. Your comfort is our delight."

I groaned.

"Oh, it won't be for long," she said. "Not if you play ball. You will admit that, as far as you were concerned, the honor system was a bust."

I sighed the sigh of a wimp caught between a rock and a hard case.

"Don't worry," she said, squeezing my thigh again, "in Switzerland we are very progressive. We allow conjugal visits in jail."

I gasped. She laughed.

When we got to headquarters, a brownish brick affair that bespoke the dead seriousness of the Swiss, I looked up the stone steps and saw some trusty inmate sweeping them like Swiss cuckoo clockwork.

Inside I was given the red-carpet criminal treatment. Neither the desk man who booked me nor the uniformed

166

sap that took my portrait and did the schtick with the finger-prints seemed too happy in his work.

When they started to put the leg irons on me, I yelped.

"Hold still," the uniform said.

"Jane!" I yelled.

"Calm down, fella," he said, but Jane showed up on the other side of the bard. "Max, do we have to do that? Mr. Stark is a gentleman."

"Regulations," he said.

"Let's make an exception."

He shook his head. "No can do. You get a signed order from the captain, okay."

"I will," she said.

"Captain'll be back Monday," he said, showing some wayward teeth.

"Oh, dear." She seemed put out. Of course it was bogus and an insult besides, but I said nothing. "Will it be too terribly uncomfy, Gil?" she asked with mock sympathy.

I didn't respond.

"The thing is, we're a little understaffed and we can't handle all the prisoners in the lockup without this cruel arti-ficial barrier to escape. Not that anyone would suspect you of escaping, Gil," she said. "You can hardly be held account-able for leaving my place. I quite understand your confu-sion."

With the chains in place I thought my humiliation complete. But, no, I was led into a cozy cell with a tiny win-dow near the ceiling. The opening was big enough for a tod-dler to squeeze through—maybe.

It had bars on it.

I was led in there by Al or Hans, I could no longer tell them apart. Without a word, I was pushed down in one of those straight wooden chairs that the Salvation Army thinks twice about picking up. I could not remember a more uncomfortable chair in my lifetime. Fortunately.

He left me alone for what seemed an eternity. For everything there is a season, the Bible says. If so, this seemed to be the time to die.

Instead it was the time they left the suspects alone to sweat it out. To consider all their options even before they were given. To make up a story and try and stick with it under a barrage of buttonhole-popping questions from the constabulary. It was not unusual for a suspect to sit alone in a room like this for hours. And then, on seeing the first human face enter the cell, blurt out a confession. A lot of the confessions were accurate. But not all. The police knew criminal psychology. No one knew it better.

But what did they want of me? Obviously Jane spoke of trading information. But I didn't think I had anything that would interest them. Anything they didn't already know. I decided they probably wanted to use me for entrapment. Wear a wire—get the big boys. But if there was any fraud or theft by Franklin d'Lacy, my principal, I didn't know it. He certainly gave me no indication of hanky-hanky.

Then Jane entered with her tape recorder and set it on the table between us. To her credit, she sat on the same kind of chair I did.

"Miserable chairs," she muttered. She winked at me. "Off the record."

In spite of myself, I smiled at her. She was, after all, a smashing-looking woman. I have noted before and I'll say it again: All of life is sexual repression. But not with Jane Eaton. So what chance did a little repressed guy like me have up against this goddess who could give you a time like was only known in Muslim heaven?

Speaking of police psychology, there was nothing could top putting a vulnerable guy (and what guy wasn't vulnerable?) like me in a coop with a woman like Jane Eaton. It was no contest—I'd be eating out of her lap in no time.

"Where's the bad cop?" I asked.

"I'm going to be both for a while. If I'm not bad enough, we'll call Al in. He does a beautiful adversarial."

"Brass knuckles?" I asked. "Rubber hoses?"

"Not unless absolutely necessary," she said. "Now, Gil, I'm going to turn on this little machine to record our chat. That okay with you?"

"You mean, I have a choice?"

"All life is choices, Gil. You can talk now or give it some thought while you cool your chain-inhibited heels in the hoosegow. You know, the timetable is up to you. You are in complete control."

"Thanks," I said. "Don't you have to read me some rights and offer me a lawyer or something?"

"Oh, Gil," she laughed all over the scale, "you're really something. You'd think you were in an American jail, picked up for rape or armed robbery. These are white-collar crimes we're concerned with, that's all."

If it was so unimportant, I wondered, what was I doing in the slammer in leg chains?

"We don't employ those niceties the American justice system has for ingratiating itself into the plight of the hard-core criminals. Human rights for the subhuman, we say here. Believe me, if I thought you needed a lawyer, I'd be the first to get you one."

"That's reassuring," I said.

"Good—are you ready?" she asked, her hand on the tape machine.

"One more question. Perhaps I should save it for the tape."

"What is it? We can always repeat it."

"How is it a guy who doesn't need a lawyer needs leg chains?"

She waved her hand as though that were the least significant question in the world. "I explained that was just routine procedure. It's nothing personal, Gil."

"That's *very* reassuring," I said. She turned on the recording machine.

She went through the introductory routine: Name, aliases (I was in the big time, I had one), address, occupation (I said "property manager"), an autobiographical sketch.

Then she said, "Your testimony here is being freely given, is it not?"

"If you call being locked up with leg irons freely," I

said. She frowned.

"No promises have been made to you for any specific answers, have they?"

"Well," I said, "there were strong suggestions if I cooperated, things would go easier."

Jane snapped off the machine. "Gil, Malvin, Mr. Stark, Mr. Yates—whoever you want to be—this contrary stuff is getting us nowhere. You want to fence all night or all year, it's up to you. We'll give you three meals a day and your own television. Believe me, I'm your friend."

"The good cop." I grinned.

"Yeah. Don't make me turn bad. I can be a mean mama."

I didn't doubt her.

"Now, will you just play along so I can get you out of here?" Her finger was on the button again.

"That's not making promises for specific answers?"

"No, dammit, just give us the truth." I had finally made her angry, or was this our bad cop coming to the fore?

I decided I had made my point and agreed to play along.

Then she erased the answers and last two questions and she asked them again. So much for making my point on the tape. It just pointed up how she could do anything with the tape: erase answers, alter others. I was at her mercy. As some anti-feminists would say, "When rape is inevitable, relax and enjoy it."

So I was doing pretty well, saying what she wanted me to say, telling my story from d'Lacy and Hadaad to Albert Durant, buying the paintings, Jacques Moran authenticating the Monet, and my "flight," as she insisted on calling my exit.

As I explained my fee arrangements and the million dollars in escrow in Los Angeles, she dropped her first explosive device.

"You know the Alpine Escrow Company doesn't exist."

"What are you talking about?" I protested. "How do

you know anything about a Los Angeles escrow company? There must be thousands of them."

"Hundreds anyway," she corrected me. "Gil, you know I've been through all your belongings. Surely even you must have been a little suspicious when the escrow papers you signed had no address. Only a fax number."

"I don't think that's so unusual. It was a transatlantic fax transmission. Save space, save money. I'm sure the letterhead has the whole ball of paraffin."

"Ah," she sighed, "hope *does* spring eternal in the human breast. Well, let's put it this way then," she said. "On a hunch, I checked with our Los Angeles people. There is no listing for Alpine Escrow or Lou Alpine. I suspect d'Lacy was playing with you."

"So maybe it's a new listing."

She shook her head. "No listing as of this minute."

Grasping at wheat, I said, "Maybe they're unlisted. You know, real exclusive."

"Yeah, wouldn't that be the cat's pajamas?"

"That's it? Pajamas? I always said 'cat's nightgown.'"

"They are so exclusive they seem to be in business solely for the convenience of Franklin d'Lacy," she said. I got the sense she was starting to feel sorry for me. I was touched. Sort of.

"How would you know that?" I asked.

"Because the fax number you sent your papers to is the number of the fax machine in Franklin d'Lacy's home."

"Oh, no!"

She nodded her head, sadly, and said:

"You've been conned."

24

So the guy who has a soft spot in his heart for a resourceful con man (me) has been conned. One thing about being an unheroic sort of guy (me) was you could absorb blows quickly and shrug them off, not as though I were Superman (not me) but rather some poor bloke who has lived his life on bargain-basement expectations (me) and is quite accustomed to having all kinds of wastes dumped on him.

My options seemed to be dwindling. Then I got an idea. I asked Jane if I could make a phone call.

"Sure. As many as you want. Of course, we'll ask you to pay for them. And I might want to listen in. Any trouble with that?"

"No," I said, trying to convince myself that it didn't bother me to have Big Sister hovering over my every word.

"Who do you want to call first?"

"d'Lacy," I said. "I want to confront him with the escrow business—maybe I can get something out of him."

"Good. Maybe you can get something for us."

"Like what?"

"Oh, like he'll tell you he's going to defraud the insurance company. Get as many details as you can. You play ball with us, we'll play with you."

I was very much afraid she was *already* playing with me.

"Before we go to the phone," I said, "can you tell

me how you got involved in this thing, and what you've done?"

"Glad to," she said, pausing for the emphasis. "Of course, if you are privy to our case, you will only have two options."

"What are they?"

"You stay in jail until we solve the case, or two, you work with us until we solve it."

I shook my head. "I don't want to hear anything," I said. "Your price is too high."

"Well, hold your ears," she said, "I'm going to tell you anyway."

I held my ears. She moved her lips without saying anything. I know because my fingers over my ears were splayed apart.

"Because," she added, "whether I tell you or not, the same conditions apply. The only way you get out until the case is disposed of is to cooperate."

"Does that mean I'd have to give up my fee?"

"Not necessarily," she said, "I suppose you may have a lawful contract. But the object is unlawful, so it's doubtful. But I won't make that any of my concern. Though I wouldn't be optimistic about getting a fee from Alpine Escrow or the guy who made it up. For verily I say unto you, you cannot get honey from lemons."

"What about Moran? He offered me a million."

"Sure, and I expect he was counting on the same insurance scam as d'Lacy. But now that Jacques Moran saw I was onto the plot, I think you'll find him laying low with the profile. Did you see the perspiration on his forehead when I was talking to you? It was deep enough to float a battleship."

She was right. About Moran, about me. She had me. For nice as a stay in this ultra-clean slammer with conjugal visits from Miss Swiss Movement might be compared to the compost heap of Tyranny Rex's bed and board (I'll bet even the food here in jail is better than Tyranny's), I would miss my palm trees too much. Not being able to monitor their minuscule growth daily was a real dragon for me. So what the heck, I thought, let's hear Jane's story.

I noticed she carefully turned off the tape recorder before she began her story. I smiled at the action. She paid me no heed.

"How many of us could resist turning an easy, undetectable favor for five million dollars?" she began. "For isn't art an illusion, after all? What makes a painting by a deranged Dutchman, who never sold a painting in his life, worth fifty-two million dollars? If a living man could paint the exact painting so close to the original that certified experts could be fooled, what would that forgery be worth?"

I shrugged my shoulders but Jane wasn't looking for a reaction.

"I don't know," I said.

"Would a Durant forgery of a Van Gogh in Van Gogh's lifetime be worth anything? Of course not. So, by extrapolation, if you can't tell a work is a forgery and you are willing to pay, say, sixteen million for it, is it worth it?"

"Well, it is to you," I said. "If you're willing to pay."

"Yes, but suppose you aren't buying the art itself but the scarcity of a name artist who has proven through the marketplace adept at commanding astronomical prices for his work. Then what is your reaction when you discover your beautiful painting was done by a contemporary forger and was never touched by Monet at all?"

"Anger."

"Yes, and what do you do?"

"Call the police," I said.

"Do you? Think about it. What do you gain? The satisfaction of seeing some poor artist sap, perhaps a dealer or two behind bars? What happens to your painting and your sixteen million dollars in the meantime? They become instantly worthless. Much better, you decide, to keep the nuisance quiet, stoutly maintain you bought an original, not a fake, and you had it authenticated. So what's the point of going to the police? Going to the cops brands the work a fake. So you sit tight."

I nodded. She seemed pleased.

"We are in this rarefied atmosphere, don't forget. The stratosphere of scams. All the principals have giant egos. It is one of the toughest crimes to prosecute because no one wants to admit they were duped. Makes them look foolish. Stupid."

She looked up at me with her provocative eyes. "So," she asked, "are you feeling sorry for me yet?"

"Maybe if you had the leg chains," I said.

"Oh, Gil, believe me, if the captain were here, you wouldn't have them."

"Very reassuring," I said.

"You're a good sport," she said, as though saying it would make it so. "So, you know what happens when you water these big egos?"

"Water?"

"They grow. So here we have d'Lacy, on the ropes at his museum. Thinks he needs something flashy. Lives from media hype to media hype. Last inquiring reporter wanted to know why LAMMA lagged behind in acquisitions. It set him thinking Albert Durant. The genius and the patsy. He supplies the talent and walks away with less than one percent of the prize."

"But I thought he was on your side?"

"Yes, now. We gave him the option of jail, like we're giving you. He'd decided to cop a plea as a friendly witness. Then there's Hadaad. A snake, in my book. He slinks from victim to victim, poisoning them with his fangs. In this case he's the buyer and the seller. He puts up half—about eight million—and suckers the museum to put up the other half. He receives all the credit and a delightful tax deduction for his efforts, then collects the eight million as his half of Jacques Moran's operation. Of course, he is a blind partner with some tax haven to stash the cash. So his eight million donation costs him around five million after taxes, and he reaps eight million, tax free, on the other end. A nice three million profit."

"d'Lacy knows all this?"

"Be deaf, dumb and blind if he didn't," she said. "But something went wrong. A nice, sensible, profitable plan went awry. The painting was switched."

"Why should they care? It seems the painting was incidental to the operation you described."

"Yes, if they'd received it. Or even another passable copy. But what they got was an embarrassing, obvious forgery. Now the unexpected rears its ugly head. Attention is going to be called to their sleazy deal, which might have passed unnoticed in the media—oh, maybe a column inch on the back pages saying LAMMA paid sixteen for a Monet. But no scrutiny. So they want to get the painting back in that box and return to the status quo."

"Oh. But who switched the paintings?"

"We did." She glowed like an ingenue after a standing ovation.

"But why? Why not just close in on the original? Arrest them on the spot?"

"Silly boy. Ever hear of evidence? You need evidence to convict. You don't get far on suppositions. You get evidence in these high-blown cases by stirring people up. Putting fear into them. Making deals."

"Where does Jacques Moran fit in all this?"

"Probably pretty much as he told you. Except he doesn't believe for a minute the picture is genuine. He was the one who had Albert Durant paint it in the first place."

'Why didn't you pick him up?"

"He's not going anyplace. His reputation is all-important to him."

"So why is he having Albert paint Monets for him?"

"Money. He's trying to get Hadaad out of his operation. Can you blame him?"

"Not me," I said.

"Then there's the hope he'll lead us to some other players," she said.

"How would he do that?"

"We're having him followed," she said.

"Is that ethical?" I asked. "Doesn't he have a right of

privacy?"

"He's suspected of a crime. Sometimes, I suppose, morality is a matter of expedience."

"Morality?" I said, zonked at her use of the term. "What kind of morality are you sporting, hopping from bed to bed to serve your purposes?"

"Well, holy smokes," she laughed. "And what are you calling the kettle, Mr. Pot? I understand you're married. And Sarah in between? Why, if I didn't know you better, I'd say you were some kind of alley cat."

"And who are you, the Virgin Mary?"

More laughter. "Oh, dear, no," she said, nodding her agreement with my indictment, "but why are you Americans so hung up on sex? Your movies, your television, ads, magazines, newspapers, books even. Sex, sex, sex. Why is that, Mr. Yates? Personally you repress it, publicly you're inundated. You know what I think? I think the all-pervasive sexual illusions in your society hope to assuage the deep-seated sexual repressions you all suffer. See it, dream about it, watch it, fantasize, just don't do it."

Her look was a challenge to me to present an argument.

"I can't argue," I said, "I'm sure you're right."

"Good." She had her hands on her hips as she nodded in satisfaction. "Let's go call d'Lacy," she said.

I hobbled down the corridor to an office. It was Jane's. "This one is on us," she said, dialing the operator and giving her d'Lacy's private number supplied by me. "As long as you get him on the insurance-scam subject."

I took the phone after it started to ring.

"Mr. d'Lacy?"

"Gil!"

"Did you get my escrow papers?"

"Yes, I believe the escrow company told me they had them."

"Escrow company?" I said, sounding confused. "I sent them to your home."

There was a silence while, I suppose, he tried to figure out what I knew, what part I bluffed, and what he should do. "What's that?" he bought more time.

"I sent the papers to your house."

"You did? Why?"

"Didn't you get them? That fax number was your fax number."

"Oh, perhaps I did. For convenience—expedite. Yes, I remember—well, good. When do you get here with the painting?"

"Alpine Escrow doesn't exist," I said. "I'm afraid I won't be getting there with any painting."

"Gil!" he pleaded. "We had a deal."

"Sorry. You want to wire the million to me, I'll bring the painting."

"Gil!"

"My faith has been stretched beyond the breaking port. You conned me. Not only don't you have the money, the painting is a fake."

"Gil! That painting is not a fake. We paid sixteen million for it!"

"To who? Hadaad?"

"You got it wrong, Gil. Hadaad was the buyer."

"And seller, as it turned out. Nice trick."

"Gil, will you bring me the painting as you agreed?" His tone was icier now.

"The money...as you agreed?"

"I told you I'd get you the money. I need the painting first."

"Sorry, you lied to me before. There's a saying in law, *falsus in uno, falsus in omnibus*." Jane was waving her hand to encourage me to hit pay dirt. "So how will you get the money, if you have the painting?" I asked as though I were genuinely, if warily, interested.

"I told you, Gil. There are ways."

"What ways?"

"Insurance companies that insured it. They don't want to spend sixteen million. They'd be happy to spend less. A couple million, maybe, to restore the work to its

178

rightful owner."

"But suppose it really is a fake?"

"Ah, there's your convincing argument. If we thought there was the slightest chance it was a fake, would we be trying to get it back? Just let the insurance company pay off. But we really want that painting," d'Lacy said. "I want it for my museum."

"Well," I said, "it sounds too chancy to me. The guy that bought the painting in the first place is going to buy it again, albeit at a greatly reduced price, and sell it to the insurance company so they can give it back to him. They go for that stuff, do they?"

"Well, of course I wouldn't negotiate directly."

"Third party?"

"Exactly."

"How about this? *Tell* the insurance company you need a million up front to get the painting back, then another million, or whatever you want, to seal the deal. You'd have your painting, I'd have my promised fee, the insurance company would save fourteen mil, and everybody would be happy as clamshells."

"Well, Gil, of course you have the painting, you could deal with the insurance company direct. Sell it to them for a million. They'll be grateful for the easy deal."

"No, thanks," I said, "I told you scamming the insurance company wasn't my box."

"Bag," he said. "'Not my bag' is the way that saying goes." He sounded so weary. "I'll see what I can do, Gil," he said. "Keep in touch."

Jane gave me the touché sign, with the circled thumb and forefinger.

I didn't know what she was so happy about. I just killed my deal.

25

I was exhausted talking to d'Lacy as a police spy. I felt I had been drawn and quartered, or maybe even half-dollared.

When I'd finished with d'Lacy and hung up the phone, Jane gave me a hug. "Good boy," she said.

Can you be touched and demeaned at the same time?

"Here," she said, standing up, "let me show you your room. We can talk more there if you like—or you can rest awhile and I'll come back later."

"My room?" I said. "What a delightful way to put it."

"What would you call it?" She seemed surprised.

"At home we say cell."

"Well, come and see. Then you can call it what you like."

We went down the short hallway, then turned to a longer one where we passed rows of doors like you'd find in an apartment building. She took a key and opened one of them, about halfway down. The inside of the room looked like a college dormitory room. A single with a fairly narrow steel bed, a chair and a desk to do some late-night studying for that English lit. exam—or, I suppose, a Swiss lit. exam here. If that's not an anachronism. Swiss history maybe. I had to admit it was nicer and more commodious than the Green Hotel, but it didn't have a palm tree to make me feel at home.

"Why, this looks like a dorm room," I said to Jane. I was trying to be appreciative. "There's even a table to study Swiss history."

She laughed. "An easy course if there ever was one. Neutrality in wars doesn't fill history books. You've heard the comparison, of course, with our southern neighbor?"

"No."

"Italy was plagued with centuries of wars, subjugation from invasions, ravishment of the countryside by enemy forces. One devastation after the other. Yet they gave the world Leonardo da Vinci, Michelangelo, Giuseppe Verdi, the Sistine Chapel, St. Peter's, one of the world's great religions. Switzerland, on the other hand, has enjoyed centuries of peace and tranquility, and what have they contributed to the world? The cuckoo clock."

Jane, when all was said and gone, was an amusing woman. "That was in a movie," she said. "*The Third Man,* I believe it was called. Isn't that great?" She seemed to get a special kick out of putting her country down. I knew a lot of people like that at home, but their put-downs were not graced with Jane's humor.

Jane sat on the bed and put both hands beside her and pressed them into the mattress. "Pretty good bed," she announced. "A little tight for two perhaps, but the presidential suite is occupied. If it opens up, I'll recommend you for it."

I sat in the straight-backed desk chair and looked across about two feet of floor at her.

There we sat, with the door unlocked, just she and I—no guards anywhere in sight. What if I just stood up and overpowered her and walked out of here? It was a testament to my stature that the thought hadn't occurred to her. Or maybe it was her deep and abiding faith in leg chains.

"Well, Gil, or Malvin, as the case may be." She spoke with a peculiar insouciance. "Since you're going to be Switzerland's guest here for a while, I don't see what I have to lose finishing my story. Then you can decide if you want to join us or fight us."

She had a unique way of characterizing my situation—a unique woman, no doubt about it.

"We had been watching Albert Durant for some time. He is, of course, a genius of art impersonation. Best in the world. He's done time, you know. A real tragedy, because in a real sense he's the victim."

"Victim?"

"Yes—of his talent. Of rich and greedy criminals-at-heart. The rich who want to get richer. When you are starving, it isn't easy to say no to fifty or a hundred thousand dollars. So we went to Albert in his garret and made him a proposition."

"We?"

"I. We would move him into a villa in the hills above Zurich. I believe you visited him there."

"Yes."

"He would just have to keep us apprised of any approaches made to him for forgeries. And in exchange for his room and board he would agree not to solicit business for forgeries, nor to paint and try to pass off as originals any forged paintings. It was a nice deal for him, and for us it was less expensive than keeping Albert in jail."

"No!" I said.

"Yes. Just in case he wasn't as forthcoming as we might hope, we bugged the place."

"But isn't that illegal?"

"There you go again, knocking yourself out for the criminal. Fraud is illegal; forgery is illegal. Both are worse than a little invasion of privacy."

"So who made contact with Albert?"

"Hadaad. Who else? We have a saying here: Wherever obscene amounts of money are to be made illicitly, Michael Hadaad cannot be far away."

"Surely that's an exaggeration?"

"Of course. But he was there all right, suborning fraud and forgery, and we got it all on tape."

"So why didn't you arrest him?" I asked.

She shook her head. "It's not enough. So many ways a weasel like Hadaad can weasel out of that. Taping is illegal, as you pointed out. He could say he wasn't really asking him to forge, merely to paint 'like' Monet. Juries give the benefit of the doubt. But it was a good start. The order was for an original Monet to be found in an attic. So it would be a painting not cataloged, so no direct comparisons could be made. Albert was quite excited. Monet was one of his favorites. He'd always wanted to do the flag thing, so he blended it with a couple other paintings–including another artist—Childe Hassam—who did a lot of flags. The result was quite striking. Well, you've seen it."

"How did Jacques Moran get involved?"

"Hadaad had muscled in on his gallery. Art market was in a slump and the vulture was looking to find a foothold where he could wheel and deal."

"Wheel and steal?" I said.

"Deal. But, no, on second thought, yours is the more apt description. The painting was made; Moran provided the bogus provenance. d'Lacy was looking for a coup—pick-me-up—for his Los Angeles museum, and Hadaad volunteered to pick up half the tab—for the aforementioned three mil tax break."

"Why would d'Lacy take a risk like that?"

"d'Lacy's ego is so oversized he thought all he would have to do is pronounce the work a genuine, long-lost Monet and the art world would accept it as so. If he failed, he would still have the nice six-million-dollar cushion to retire on. He'd been having some squabbles with his board over his pension, so he thought why not take his own? The LAMMA board was getting ready to can him anyway. We just hastened the process by switching the painting to an embarrassing forgery."

"Why were they going to fire d'Lacy?"

"Oh, you know him. He wears thin after a while. You get worn out with all that hype and self-promotion. It's like staring into the midday sun. It's spectacular all right, but how much can you take?"

"So why did d'Lacy hire me?"

She looked at me with a tilted head and a crooked smile. Trying, it seemed, to understand just how naive I could be. "You don't know?"

I shrugged to make it look like maybe I did know. "I'd like your slant on it," I said.

"You are the ultimate low-profile detective. Only one other case. They couldn't go to an established, legitimate agency, they were breaking the law and the big boys don't put up with that. Ditto the cops. If it was such a legitimate art purchase, why not report it to the cops?"

"d'Lacy told me it was a political matter within his board. Didn't want any publicity."

"That too. But for other reasons as well. He'd bilked the board by buying a forgery. Of course, it was a good one. The best money could buy. Albert Durant knows how to make them pass all the age tests. He really is a genius at his game, you know. So I could foresee the international controversy surrounding forgery number one outliving d'Lacy himself. So we threw an obvious fake into the soup. *Any*one would know it was a fake. So d'Lacy wanted to get the real fake back before anyone caught on. He kept telling everyone the Monet hadn't arrived yet."

"But what made him think I could retrieve the other one?"

"Not that hard really. Shouldn't be, anyway, for a guy who found Hadaad's daughter. The art world in this stratosphere is small and provincial. What did it take you— not exactly a seasoned professional, if you will pardon my saying so? Four, five days?"

"About that. But what if I hadn't met your friend Sarah?"

Jane grinned. "I have a lot of friends in the art world. They all know my relationship with Albert Durant. Sooner or later someone would have sent you my way. Might have added a couple days, that's all." She stood up and stretched her arms to the ceiling, her mufti doing things to her storybook body (*adult* books) that I am not a seasoned enough writer to adequately describe.

"Yes or no?" she said.

"Yes or no what?"

"Are you for us, or again' us?"

"I'd never be again' you," I said.

"Good. Does that mean you're coming aboard?"

"What does that mean to me?"

"We drop the charges, for starters," she said.

"Charges?"

She nodded. "Stealing evidence. Flight. Lots of stuff."

"Oh, my," I said, sinking down in a chair so hard that was impossible. But I just felt my body shrinking to accommodate the news.

"So you continue your work for d'Lacy—you're almost home–only you continue it for us. You may have to put him off a bit while we wire you up with recorders and pump Hadaad and d'Lacy until we can make our case."

"Couldn't that be dangerous?"

"Walking across the street can be dangerous," she said.

"*You* did that? Tried to have me run down?"

"That was Phillipe. He's a world-class stunt driver. He wouldn't have touched you—"

"But he did," I said. "I was knocked over."

"No. You touched him," she said. "Tsk, tsk, it taught you a lesson, didn't it? You are *very* careful in the streets now. Aren't you?"

I admitted I was, though I didn't think much of the lesson and told her so.

"But it is a lasting memory of what we could do if we wanted to," she said. "Am I right?"

I just glared at her—my real tough-guy glare. Jane was taking shape as a power-mad monster and I didn't like it.

"So—what do you say?"

"If that's a taste of what I'm in for, I say no."

"That's a taste of what you're in for if you say no,"

she said, drilling her eyes into mine.

"I've got an awful lot invested in this to give up my fee."

"What hope of that fee can you possibly still have?"

"The insurance money?" I offered meekly as a mild question.

"You think the cops on this case would sit idly by while you–or someone on your behalf—defrauded the insurance company? That's what we're trying to avoid here."

"But if it trapped them? I mean, it would be pretty good evidence against them if we went through it all, fee and everything."

"And you think you could *keep* the fee? You think when someone gives an undercover cop fifty thousand dollars to make a hit, he gets to *keep* the money?"

"There has to be some way," I said.

She shook her head. "Not if you're with us. And if you aren't with us, you're in here." She stretched again. I wanted to keep her there talking so she'd keep stretching, but she said, "Think it over. I'll be back in the morning for your answer" And with one more stretch, followed by her bending over to kiss me square on the lips (her lips were the rain forest), she was gone. I heard the key turn in the door lock.

Left alone to ponder my fate, or mortality, as the case might be, my thoughts stuck on Jane. My fate seemed to be in her hands. Yet she was a dream figure. Every man's ideal. A gorgeous girl who happily, and with apparent personal enjoyment, jumped in bed with you. There was no demand, or even seeming desire, to push a "relationship." You didn't even have to take her to lunch.

Tyranny Rex, on the other hand, was the woman for whom was coined the phrase "conjugal *duty*." In my heyday she would pepper intimacy with such endearments as "You again." and "Didn't we just do this?"

I remember how we were forever saving it for marriage. Well, you'd think with all that saving there would have been not only a lot of principal saved up, but generous interest as well.

Huh-uh. Jane, on the other hand, would probably laugh me out of town (I should be so lucky) if I even mentioned marriage.

It was after midnight when I finally drifted off to sleep and was jarred awake by the key in the door. It was pitch black when the door closed. Without a word, a woman got in bed with me. It didn't take me long to realize it was a woman. My next thought was anything could happen in this crazy place. I was so hoping it was Jane.

It was.

26

As quickly as Jane materialized in my cell, she made as fleet an exit. A few hours later, not long after the sun came up, Jane returned to my cell.

"I have good news and bad news," she said. "Good news first. Someone called the insurance company and said they could produce the missing Monet for two million. One million up front, the other on delivery. A photograph would be delivered to verify its authenticity."

"Good," I said. Of course, I hadn't heard the bad news.

"Bad news is the insurance company refused." She chuckled. I'm so glad she could take some humor from my plight.

"It was very nice of you to pay me a visit last night," I said with a sheepish gratitude. I don't know why, when I was riding in the fast lane, I had to act like I was peddling a bicycle in low gear. I guess you can't teach an old dog new routines.

"How'd you know it was me?" she asked, skewing her pretty features just so, and dropping, unceremoniously, to the bed.

"I recognized your earrings."

"I wasn't wearing any." She lay back on the bed. So languidly and...provocatively.

"Oh," I said. "I suppose you were across town checking on a box of pastels belonging to a guy who does some beautiful Pissarros."

"Oh, you know Pissarro?"

"Not personally. His ex-wife used to date our house-keeper's stepson," I said. "Or was that Picasso?"

"Probably Rembrandt," she said.

"I've heard of him too."

"Well, enough intellectual pursuit," she said. "Are you with us or not?"

"I've been thinking," I said, putting my chained bare feet up on the bed.

"Oh, dear," she said, reaching out to wiggle my toes with her fingers. "I was so hoping we could avoid that."

"Oh?" I didn't really understand what she meant.

"Every time you think, Gil, it hurts the ball club."

We both laughed, she perhaps harder than I. An ordinary guy might have been insulted, but I was so accustomed to verbal abuse from a towering, glowering, tyrannical female that it ran off me like dewdrops off a duck's sacroiliac.

I told her what I was thinking anyway. My plan to salvage my fee and do my duty to Interpol—and, coincidentally, get me out of the hoosegow.

Her pretty face became less pretty as we spoke. It took on a lot of the wrinkles of skepticism and wariness.

"Are you really that hard up for a few dollars?"

"Can we just say that a million to me is not 'a few' dollars?" I said. "Not that I shouldn't some day aspire to share your pathological disdain for money." You know, I may not have said exactly that. These high-blown phrases don't often just roll off my tongue like that. They are more often the product of a lot of brooding hindsight.

"Sorry," she said, but she wasn't. "If I get your drift, Gil, you want the police to turn a blind eye while you extort a million dollars under false pretenses."

"Not so. I have an agreement, a contract."

"Verbal?"

"All right," I admitted. "Verbal. I am honoring the contract, and they will be happy to pay." I couldn't admit d'Lacy had made a few written notes, because I don't remember what happened to them.

"When they realize I am right behind to confiscate the work?"

"Look at it this way. They have bilked millions from innocents. Why shouldn't they give me a small percentage of it? I've done my part—spent a lot of time and money—I should be paid."

"Two wrongs make a right?"

That required no answer—not that I had a good one. We sat in silence while she concentrated on twiddling my toes. Finally she heaved a heavy sigh that did marvelous things for the pink-sweater-encased glandular attachments to that upper part of her anatomy.

"Are you telling me," she asked, "unless we cooperate with you, you won't cooperate with us?" She nodded her head vigorously. I just stared at her. She repeated the action, then pulled up her sweater to reveal the wire recording device strapped to her abdomen.

"Yes," I said, resounding in the cell as though it were an echo chamber.

"You mean you're willing to sit here indefinitely if we won't go along with you?"

Again her vigorous nod. Again my resounding "Yes." I'd bet if I got to hear that tape I sounded like Sly Stallone.

"You realize you could be charged with a crime?"

"Yes."

"Tried, convicted and jailed?"

"Yes." I was beginning to sound like Molly Bloom in the end of *Ulysses*.

"Phew," she said. "Then I guess we don't have much choice." She reached under her sweater to turn off the machine. "You drive a hard bargain." She smiled.

"A lot of people tell me that," I said.

Then she laid down her own ground rules. Of course, they were impossible, but what choice did I have? As she pointed out, they *could* let me sit there until hair grew under my toenails. It was a delightful expression. I hadn't heard it before and, actually, I'm not sure I remembered it correctly. Hair on a cue ball perhaps?

To start the sphere rolling, as they say, Jane led me to the telephone, where I called Jacques Moran. Poor man was waiting in his hotel, terrified that the police were going to pick him up.

"I don't think you're in jeopardy," I said. "Not if you cooperate." A nice touch, I thought, though not exactly authorized by the authorities.

"Cooperate?" His voice quavered. "What do I have to do?"

"Have you told anyone about the police intervention in this matter?"

"No," he said so abruptly I believed him.

"Good," I said. "Could you drop over here for a chat?" I asked.

"With whom?"

"Me."

"You alone?"

"Yes."

"Where?"

I gave him the address. "Ask for me at the desk. They'll show you to my room."

"Room? They didn't lock you up?" He breathed an excited breath. "I thought you were a goner for sure. Looked pretty heavy at the airport. Are you telling me you're at liberty?"

"Not exactly. I'll tell you when you get here."

"Suppose I don't come?"

"Same treatment I got at the airport."

"Oh."

"Want me to send the goons?"

"No, no, I'll be right there."

And he was. He must have taken a rocket to get there so quickly.

The best news was they took off my leg irons for the meeting. I let Moran take the chair and I sat on the bed. I was sure the place was bugged, and I realized they were get-

191

ting enough on me to keep me there for eons. But I had to give it the old adult-education try.

Jacques Moran was not at ease in my "room." He kept looking around as though he expected any minute to be attacked by killer termites.

"What *is* this place?" he asked.

"My dorm room."

"Oh. You're in school?"

"In a way."

"Just happens to be in a police station?" he said.

"But an up-market one, wouldn't you say?"

He didn't say.

"I've asked you here to solicit your help in a matter of mutual concern for our mutual benefit. I am acting on the assumption that you would not be brokenhearted to surgically remove Michael Hadaad from your operation."

The gasp I heard was all the answer I needed.

"Good."

"But," he sputtered, "but, how would you be able to do that? I can't buy him out. I don't have the funds."

"So what happened to your share of the sixteen million?"

"But I thought you knew. Franklin d'Lacy took six million, Hadaad took eight and I got two. But out of mine came all the expenses, including a million-dollar loan payment to Hadaad. Coming to Zurich is never cheap. I had to escape the Hadaads. I had to get the painting back—my reputation—"

"But what kind of reputation do you have if the work is a fake?"

"d'Lacy is a museum curator. He says it's genuine. What is my opinion next to that? He says I am responsible for the switch. They have promised to ruin me unless I get the picture back." He seemed to be breaking down. "I was going to try to make a little, I'll admit, selling it to the insurance company."

I guess I was looking a little too hard at him, because he offered me an unexpected explanation.

"You don't have to give me a disapproving look. It is done *all* the time. Insurance companies expect it. It's built into their premiums. Much more economical to give me two or three million than pay LAMMA sixteen."

"Who insured it?"

"Lloyd's. And you know what trouble they're in. Their investors are covering their losses personally. So I should expect two or three would be a welcome gift when the prospect of sixteen is staring you in the face."

"Does ethics come into play here in any way?"

He seemed to disappear into the suit he was wearing. He dropped his head into his hands and the big draught of air he sucked in ended in a short sob. "I'm so ashamed," he said. "I often think, what would my mother say? I had an impeccable reputation, then I got in with Hadaad, that snake. He swallowed me whole. I've been standing on quicksand ever since. My only goal in life is to get that albatross off my neck. Nothing else matters to me. Nothing!" He pounded his pink fist on the desk.

"Maybe I can help you."

He looked at me in a daze. "Help?" he choked on the word. "If you could get rid of that barracuda, I'd gladly change places with you here."

"I've got an idea along those lines," I said.

He shook his head. "I'll never do it. The art market has gone to hell in a handbasket and every day I get deeper in debt to Hadaad. Soon there won't be enough money in the exchequer to buy him out. I've worked a lifetime to build that gallery. It has my *name*! Now it's degenerated into a front for art fraud. Quick-buck Hadaad. A man with a pathological gluttony for the almighty dollar."

I nodded. He was certainly talking about the Michael Hadaad I knew.

"I have a plan, Mr. Moran," I said in a nice cadence, "where Mr. Hadaad would be pleased to sell your share back to you..."

Moran shook his head excitedly. "I could never do it. I told you—I just don't have the pounds."

"In my plan, Hadaad sells to you very cheaply."

Jacques Moran stared at me, his mouth agape just a tad, as if trying to figure what share of his gullibility portfolio he dared invest in that belief.

Then I told him what I wanted him to do.

27

At four-thirty sharp, Jane let me out to call Franklin d'Lacy in Los Angeles.

Franklin, bless him, almost always answered my phone calls.

"Gil?" The bombast that was d'Lacy's trademark had waned and he sounded rather forlorn.

"Mr. d'Lacy?" I wasn't sure it was the same guy.

"I guess I owe you an apology," he said. "The phony escrow was a dirty trick. But it is not to convey any disrespect for you and your work, but rather is a measure of how desperate I have become. It does me no honor. Believe me, if I had the million, I would gladly give it to you simply for your trouble. But now..." he trailed off.

"Now what?"

"Oh, I don't know." The lackadaisical persona he had taken on was so pronounced, I pictured him talking to me prone on a couch. "I'm afraid I'm through here."

"By choice?"

"Oh, no." It was a hollow sound that came through the intercontinental phone lines. "The board is meeting tomorrow night. They have accused me of the most horrendous crimes and misdemeanors. Malfeasance in office. Oh," he groaned, "it's just too painful to talk about."

"How much support have you left?"

"Hadaad's about it now, I'm afraid. And he's out of the country."

"What is the other side's case?"

"Oh, you don't want to know. Someone has put a bug in their rears that I spent sixteen million on a fake Monet."

"Lot of people here say it's a forgery."

"Yes, yes, I know."

"Could you have been fooled?"

"It's a magnificent painting, Gil," he said valiantly. "I'm sure I could convince them of that, if only..."

"What?"

"If only I had the painting to show them."

"Does that mean you are acknowledging that the work was not painted by Monet, no matter how magnificent it is?"

"Gil, Gil, you mustn't be an art snob. Look at the great Rembrandt. Half his stuff was done by his pupils. Do we turn up our noses at it because of that? And how about Rodin? Lot of student work in those magnificent bronzes. What is important, after all, the work of art itself or the person who created it?"

"Well, Mr. d'Lacy," I said, "I've gotta say I agree with you. If Jones can paint like Picasso, and Smith like Pissarro, and you can't tell them apart..."

"Exactly!" he said, starting to show signs of his prior self. "And I could make the case too," he said, "if I only had the painting."

"You mean you could convince your board?"

"College try," he said, then deflated. "Probably wouldn't do diddly to those old fogies. Art snobs to the core—every last one of them—and you know the funny thing about that?"

"No."

"They don't know a damn thing about art. About what makes just a painting a work of art. This Monet is a work of art, but, oh, if someone hints Monet might not have painted it himself, they're off and running in ersatz mock indignation to cry from the highest rooftop 'Fake!' They couldn't possibly stop to consider the work might be *better* than Monet could have done himself. Like Rembrandt's pupils. These snobs have steel-trap minds. Please don't confuse them with reason."

I was feeling truly sorry for him. "So you think it might help if you had the painting?"

The silence was prolonged. I could hear rattling breathing, but little else. "I wouldn't feel right, Gil," he said, the weight of his magnanimity fairly crushing him. "We had an agreement. I couldn't keep my end."

He sounded so pathetic, I almost wanted to give him the painting. If it had been mine to give, and I guess the fact that I was the guest of the Swiss government was fairly demonstrable proof that they, at least, didn't think it was.

And while I had a hope of turning a buck in the scheme, I didn't think I should be too foolhardy. What with my daily expenses eating away at my palm-and-cycad fund from the last case.

"I have an idea," I said. "It might solve both our problems."

"Oh, Gil. I just don't know but what my problem isn't beyond solving."

"Here's my plan. Reject it if you want," I said. "I am constantly being watched by the authorities here. I have access to the painting. I think I could get it to someone in Zurich. I tried to get it out of the country and they stopped me."

"They?"

"The authorities. The police. I don't have much time. Do you think Hadaad could come over here and get it?"

"You saw him in London, you say?"

"But I don't know if he's still there," I said. "Did you know he was half owner of Jacques Moran's gallery?"

"No!"

"So over half the sixteen million went to him. He gets a tax break for the donation, gets nine million here, including a million paydown of Moran's note, and hides it in a tax haven."

"Well I'll..." d'Lacy couldn't go on.

"So this could be the time to test his mettle. What do you say?"

"I'm speechless," he said. "I thought he had an interest in art. I thought he supported what I was doing. I thought he was sympathetic to my experiment."

"Experiment?"

"To put my theory to the test. Pay enough for a work and have some art authorities give it their stamp, and the work becomes what you say it is."

"You don't think all that's a little sophisticated for Hadaad?"

"I don't know," he said, carefully measuring his words. "I didn't think so—but now—I'm not sure. It certainly looks like this was an opportunity for him to scam some money."

"His strong suit," I said. "So do you have any objection if I try to get the fee from him—give him the painting and let him run with it?"

There was a long silence. Do you believe you can hear someone thinking? On the telephone? After that silence, I'd swear to it.

"'Let him run with it,'" he said, mulling over the words with some amusement. "That's very good, Gil. Let him run with it. The bastard sold me out. Let him run with it, he might get shot in flight."

"So I have your okay?"

"Go for it," he said.

28

So I was going to confront my old nemesis again. Like Superman had Lex Luthor and Batman had the Joker. I had Michael Hadaad.

Perhaps I should mention again that this was not his real name. It's not because I fear repercussions that I've given him a pseudonym so far off from his real name, it is rather that I am terrified of him.

He was both my client and my adversary in my first case, and he was about to kill me rather than pay my fee. I would be foolish to expect any gentler treatment this time.

Why do it? The mountain climbers say, "I climbed it because it was there," so I made my last stand for my fee with Hadaad because he was there. And he had the money. Willie Sutton always said the reason he robbed banks was that's where the money was. But I didn't consider what I was doing robbery. Others might disagree.

One advantage of having the same adversary, you knew what to expect. Or at least you have less excuse for being taken by surprise, as I was the last time.

One more check with the home front. Tyranny Rex seemed in fine fettle. Yes, my palm trees were still there. How did she know? The sun still didn't reach the windows.

She gave me a rundown on every glass-figurine sale she had for the next two months and failed to ask about my trip.

I asked if I had gotten my notice of the next Palm

Society meeting in the mail.

"I don't remember," she said. "I put all your mail in one pile, so you can look when you get here. I just made the cutest jumping horse. Stands on its hind legs, and I've got the fence too." She kept talking, but I was thinking about my palms, and our next Palm Society meeting in Malibu.

Check into any plant society, see what you find. There are jillions of them—not only palms, but bromeliads, fuchsias, cactus and succulents, bamboo, rare fruit (whose membership we delight in referring to as "rare fruits"), fern, native plants, rose, antique rose—if you've seen the plant, they've got a society. Check in and you'll find the membership from the "You're looking good" (miracle of miracles at *your* age) strata of society (childhood, youth, middle age and "You're looking good"). The theory, not widely disputed, is the older sports are into eternal life. And since things don't always look so good for the heavenly inclined, or faith in reincarnation wavers, there are always plants. Plants that we know will outlast us. The real hard core among us will plant some of those old fossil plants like the ginkgo tree or palms and cycads—trees with millions of years on them—because we want our reach to stretch longer than any mere writer or painter could hope to achieve.

After a lot of footsie with Madeline, the dragon lady at the Jacques Moran Gallery in London, Michael Hadaad came to the phone. He was as brusque as a man who realized how important he was in the scheme of things and how *un*important I was.

"I have spoken to my client Franklin d'Lacy," I began without undue pleasantries, "and he has given me permission to negotiate with you for the return of the painting."

"Why?"

"First, he doesn't have the fee."

"What did he offer you?"

"A million dollars."

He gasped.

"Apparently it was worth it to him," I said. "He

mentioned his reputation, his position, and, coincidentally, hinted that the insurance company might pay a great deal more for it."

"Then why aren't you dealing with the insurance people?" he wanted to know.

"Well, I meant to honor my commitment first. Of course, if you have no interest, that would be my next choice."

"But why not your first choice? If you could at least double that amount, and I've no reason to suppose you can't? You're not an altruist, are you?"

"Nor am I a man who scams insurance companies. I didn't steal the painting. If I sold it to them, they would have to assume that I had stolen it."

"How did you get it then?" Hadaad asked.

"I don't mind telling you all of that, once you've seen the painting, accepted it, and paid my fee."

"Certainly I shall be insisting on its recent provenance *before* I agree to any payment."

There he was again, playing the control freak. "No," I said. "Either you want the work or not. What difference does it make where it came from?"

"How do I know it's the same painting?"

"Have d'Lacy come and look at it if you like. Now we all know, do we not, that the Monet painting in question is a forgery?"

"What!" he shouted. "I know no such thing. You mean, you are going to try to sell me a forgery for a million dollars?" His tone was suspect. Knowing Hadaad as I did, my guess was he was faking it.

"No," I said, "I'm not an art expert. I was not hired to authenticate a painting but merely to retrieve the painting that was shipped to LAMMA, then removed. It is that painting I have. The one you paid half of its sixteen million purchase price. The one you received nine million dollars for as majority owner in the Jacques Moran Gallery." Then I added, "That includes a partial loan payment from Moran, I'm told."

He said nothing. The silence fairly hissed in my ears.

"Mr. Hadaad?" I inquired. I wasn't sure after all that time he was still on the line.

"I'm thinking," he said. "Suppose it were a forgery. This could be a second forgery. Why, for a small percentage of the million you could have had another made."

"I suppose, given the time and the opportunity, neither of which I've had. But you bring up an interesting point: Is a forgery of a forgery worth less than the original forgery?" I asked. "Especially if you can't tell them apart. Believe me, if there were two, I would gladly let you choose. But there is only one."

"How will I know you won't have another done, and sell that to the insurance company?"

It was a valid question. "Faith in your fellow man, I guess."

"In *you*?" he asked with a snarl.

"Now, Mr. Hadaad. Can you be objective? In our last arrangement did I not do exactly as I said I would? All your conniving to do me out of my fee was on your part."

That made him angry. "Okay, why don't you fly it to L.A.? I'll meet you there with the million and hand it over if d'Lacy says it's the Monet."

"It's not a Monet," I reminded him.

"Okay. If it's the same picture he bought."

"I guess the answer is, I'm not willing to do that. I tried to leave before and I couldn't get out of the country."

"What makes you think I could?"

"Because you are more clever and resourceful in these matters than I ever could be."

"You think I'm susceptible to that flattery?" he asked, tersely.

"I think there's a good chance."

"You have the painting in your possession?"

"Yes."

"Well, I don't suppose it can hurt to look at it."

There he was again. "No. You can't look at it. I can't risk trying to move with it more than once. Nor can I risk

202

you or your accomplices fleecing me of it."

"I don't understand. You can't leave the country with it but whoever prevented that allowed you to keep it?"

"I say it's mine. I bought it. They are trying to dispute that—so if you want to see it, bring your million in a certified check and I'll give you instructions where to meet. Interested?"

"Perhaps."

"How long to get the check?"

"An hour or two."

"All right, take it to Sarah at the gallery two doors up from Moran. She'll photocopy it and return it to you. Then take a plane to Zurich and check in the Bauer Lac Hotel. If you can't make it leave a message there for Gil Collins."

"I thought your fake name was Yates?"

"It is. But I can't be too careful. I will likewise leave further instructions for you at the desk. Of course, the same rules as last time apply. No friends. Come alone."

"You too."

"And no guns."

He hung up.

I called Sarah and asked her to fax the copy of Hadaad's million dollar check to Jane's fax.

Then a couple of the establishment's retainers showed me back to my "room."

There I sat at my economy-sized desk and pondered my strategy for my encounter with Michael Hadaad, who was slippery as a water snake, cunning as a fox, with a bite like a shark. One slip, I realized, and I could not only lose my "million-dollar" painting, but also my head.

29

Later that evening, Jane showed up in my room. She was frowning. In her hand was a fax copy. She waved it at me.

"You think this shows good judgment, Gil?"

"What is it?"

"A fax copy of a check for a million dollars made out to you."

I thought that was quite wonderful and had to suppress my excitement to match her mood.

"You don't know Hadaad," I said.

"That's not quite accurate."

"You ever do business with him?"

"Not directly."

"If you did, you'd understand why I had to see the check before I met him," I said, trying to sound apologetic. I don't think Jane was taking it that way.

"I may understand that. What I don't understand is why you felt it necessary that the whole department had access to it through the fax machine. It has taken a lot of time making feeble explanations about why one of our prisoners should be getting a million dollars. Was it for a bribe perhaps? For *you*, Lieutenant Jane Eaton? It was faxed to *your* attention, Lieutenant? What a faux pas!"

"Sorry. I didn't think. But what was I going to do? Time is, according to you, the essential. Besides, isn't this evidence? You can parade all these snoops on the witness stand to say this was received, and everybody saw it."

"Prisoners are to be seen and not heard," she said.

"Prisoners? Who's a prisoner? I thought you said I was a guest of the country."

"And so you are, strictly speaking," she said. "But with it goes a responsibility—to behave like a guest."

"Sorry," I said again, this time hanging my head to prove my contrition. Slowly, I raised my head and looked up at her standing (towering) over me. I felt like Jane was Tarzan and I was Jane. "Does this mean you won't go through with it?"

She looked at me as though I were a chastised child for whom she felt sorry. After a painful pause she said, "No. But we may have a harder time letting you have the money."

"Why?"

"Because everyone's seen this." She waved the fax again in the air and it crackled like one of those explosive breakfast cereals.

Some quick calculations shot through my mind. My wife always said anything going through my mind would meet very little resistance en route. Was Jane trying to get me to be the principal player in her sting operation for nothing? A gratis witness at the trial? Was she rather using the not inconsequential threat of further incarceration to spur me on? Where would I be without the million? My bankroll from my first coup with Hadaad was sinking below eighty grand as a result of this expensive case. I thought of the twenty-five-thousand-dollar palm I wanted to buy—and the ten- or fifteen-thousand-dollar greenhouse I'd have to build to keep it alive. Without the million, that hope would disappear as fast as a roll of coins in Las Vegas. How low could my bank balance sink before I could no longer afford to take these exotic cases on contingency? And now that I've seen these great watering holes and met these big-shot people and had these beautiful girls pursuing me as in my most remote fantasies, it will be tough to keep me content in the glass blower's factory/showroom and passing my time in boring property management as an indentured servant to

Daddybucks Wemple and Associates, Realtors.

So I screwed up my scant courage, looked up at Tarzan and said, "No money, no sting."

She looked down at me with a cocked eye. "Young man," she admonished me, "you aren't dictating to your hostess the terms of your stay, are you?"

"I couldn't say. This 'guest' stuff throws me a little. Let's just call it like it is. Might clear my head. You've got me in this jail. Okay," I said when she started to speak, "there are no bars on the doors, and one of the most beautiful women in the world pays me conjugal visits. But, nevertheless, I am restricted to my cell—ah, room. I can't come and go as I please."

"Gil, you make it sound so terrible."

"Want to trade places? Okay. Now, we make a deal. You let me see my contract through, you let me earn—and keep my fee, and I do the sting for you. Sell a purloined painting, a known forgery, to a man who has already profited illicitly from the fake. A man who will turn around and scam Lloyd's of London and profit further. Which entrapment would be a lot more suspect, a lot more difficult without my participation."

"You're backing out?"

"'S up to you," I said. "The price of my participation is the million-dollar check from Hadaad. Won't cost you a cent. Up to you."

She sighed the sigh of the frustrated, forlorn maiden she certainly was not. "I'll see what I can do," she said. "In the meantime, tell me what arrangements you made with Hadaad—for meeting, and so on."

I looked up at her. My mouth was agape.

"What's the matter?" Her eyes were in blurry focus.

"Nothing," I said. "Only I'm not giving you any more information until I get your word—in writing—that I get to keep Hadaad's check."

"*If* you get it."

"Okay, and another clause that the police will not in any way or guise keep me from getting it."

"Gil, you're getting out of line." It was a flash of anger from Jane. She had assassination in her eyes. "Police don't take kindly to prisoners dictating terms to them."

"Oh? Sorry. Then I'll just withdraw my cooperation."

"You could stay in jail for a long time."

"Oh, now it's jail, is it?" I said, waving my arm about my "room."

"You don't expect you'll stay *here* do you? No, we have real jails. Bars, the whole bit. That's where you'll be. Alone and friendless." She emphasized the last word so I could not misunderstand: There would be no late-night visits from Jane Eaton.

"I don't know." I shrugged. "I'm banking on Switzerland being the fair and reasonable country I always thought it was. Indeed, as it seems up to this moment. If you find a jury to convict a guy who wants to keep a painting he *bought and* send him to jail, then I guess I'm in the minestrone, as they say."

"Oh," she muttered, "they don't say that at all."

"That reminds me," I said, "can you get me one of those hand-held metal detectors?"

"What for?"

"To wave over Hadaad to reassure myself he doesn't have a gun or some other instrument of destruction."

"But we'll be there," she said.

"How long would it take a bullet to clean out my sinuses?"

"Fraction of a second," she conceded.

"Could you stop it?"

"Okay, I'll see what I can do," she said. Then she frowned. "Hey, how did minestrone remind you of a metal detector?"

"Minestrone has pasta in it. Pasta starts with a 'p' and so does pistol."

"Oh, my," she groaned.

Little over an hour later, Jane returned and gave me a happy wink. "It's all arranged." She smiled the smile of triumph. "I got you the metal detector," she said, as though that had been a tough assignment. "Now, where are you meeting Hadaad?"

"Nice try." I grinned.

"What do you mean?"

"What about my fee? The million?"

"Oh, that," she said, as though it were of no consequence whatever. "We don't want to know about it. Knowing about Hadaad, we have serious doubts he will be that easy to fleece, but we'll leave that part up to you. So what are your arrangements?"

"What is my remuneration?"

"I just told you..."

I shook my head. "From *you*."

"We'll see."

"We'll see? See what? Who is we? I'm not risking my life for you on speculation."

"What do you want?"

"What do you think I want? I want to get out of here. I do my job, you release me."

"Oh? And what about being a witness?"

"Hey, I'll make a statement, sign an affidavit. Agree to return to testify, anything you want. Surely you weren't thinking about holding me here until the trial?"

She pouted. "Haven't you been well treated?"

"Hey, we've been through that," I said, despairing at the turn the conversation was taking. "I should come back to the slammer and use my million to buy chewing gum?"

"What will you do with a million, Gil, *if* you get it?"

"You saw the check. It worked last time. I got a quarter of a million from the same patsy. What I do is pay my expenses, then my taxes, then some palm trees and cycads. Maybe a greenhouse. I've also been thinking of buying the house next door so I could plant it in palms. I could rent it out and have double my space."

"Palm trees, huh?" she said. "Is that normal?"

"Normal?" I said. "All I know about normal is it's overrated."

Jane left me again briefly, with the caveat "I'll be right back."

She returned with some forms and a wire device for recording conversations. I was to use it with Hadaad. She proceeded to brief me on my dialogue.

She presented me with a signed document laying out our agreement. There was a clause that any financial remuneration I received from third parties while performing this operation was mine to keep.

I would use due diligence, blah, blah, blah. The money part was all I cared about. That and the clause that said in return for my services and signed affidavit and agreement to return to testify, I would be released from my "detention."

I signed. We were all set to go. Jane and I agreed it would be best to meet Hadaad in the hotel lobby. I would leave him instructions indicating we would go somewhere after meeting, then I would ask to see the check, and when he showed it to me I would produce the painting and surprise him by making the exchange on the spot. The Interpol people would be all around—a desk clerk, a guest checking out. Jane would be in a businesslike conversation with a well-dressed gentleman. I would ask my questions and go.

They would close in. I would make a discreet, if hasty, exit from the premises with my million, and head for the nearest bank.

Then I thought perhaps I don't owe any tax. I made the money in Switzerland and stuck it in one of those convenient and notorious secret Swiss bank accounts, I just might be able to keep my foreign fee out of the clutches of Uncle Sam's revenue patrol. It could even be legal.

30

Last time for my showdown meeting with Michael Hadaad, barracuda mogul, I relied on some heavyset friends of one of the principal players. This time I would have as a backup the Swiss police and Interpol's art-fraud squad.

To minimize suspicion, we entered the lobby separately and from different directions. The guy impersonating a desk clerk came from a room behind the counter. The man checking out was stationed, with a suitcase, on Hadaad's floor (four), at the elevator. When Hadaad came down the hall, he was to push the elevator button. Then, if necessary, hold the door for Hadaad.

Jane and a plainclothes sergeant came in close behind me, and sat where they could see me. This was ostensibly for my protection. I wondered if it wasn't more to see that I didn't escape.

I had the painting wrapped in a blanket. I set it behind the counter where our ersatz clerk stood ready to help the phony checkout artist. Hadaad would come down at eight-thirty in the morning expecting to get a message at the counter from me.

The message would say I was waiting for him in the lobby. He would case the place and I would go over to greet him—then surprise him, I hoped.

The lobby was old-world gilt. The kind of place you weren't comfortable talking above a whisper.

The minute hand on the old clock barely touched

the six when the elevator door sprung open and Michael Hadaad, his countenance stern, his gait imperial, made his way to the counter, followed by the guy with the suitcase.

Hadaad was in his customary nautical outfit: blue blazer, white slacks and shoes. He even had the captain's cap with him—expecting to go out as he was.

The clerk handed him my note. He read it quickly then turned around to see me walking toward him. I held out my hand in greeting. "Mr. Hadaad," I said for the recorder, "good to see you."

"Gil," he said simply, "where are we going?"

I gave him the quick once-over with the metal detector. He jumped. "What's that?"

"Just want to make sure you're not armed."

"I'm not armed," he snapped, as though I didn't have inarguable cause for my actions, "are you?"

I ran the thing over myself. No beeps.

"Do you have the check?"

"Certainly. Where's the painting?"

"Here. May I see the check?"

"The painting?"

"Sure. Don't give me the check," I said, "just show it to me."

With that disgusted, disdainful expression that only a man of great importance can manage, and with a herculean sigh of forbearance, Michael Hadaad reached into his blue-blazer pocket and withdrew an envelope and took out the check. Holding it so tightly his knuckles turned white, he showed it to me.

It looked good to me. I nodded.

"Now, where's the painting?" he asked, replacing the check, first in the envelope, then in the pocket.

"Over here," I said, and we walked the few steps to the counter. I asked our clerk, "May I have my package, please?"

"Oh, yes, sir," he said, reaching under the counter and handing it over. I gave him a ten-franc tip. "Thank you, sir," he said. Hey, why not? I had seen my million. I was within touching distance. Maybe I should have made it twenty francs.

"This way, please," I said, leading Hadaad to a sitting area—two chairs and a low table for setting the picture down, which I did. "This painting has been very good to you, hasn't it?"

"I did all right," he said.

"What will you do with it now?"

"I don't think that's any of your business."

"I mean, I'm just curious." I used my dumbest look on him. Dumb sometimes evokes a lot more information than smart. The teaching instinct in all of us. "How do you make contact with Lloyd's without stirring up the law?"

"Insurance companies are about money, not morality," Hadaad said. "I could walk in there at ten in the morning with the painting literally on my back. They would greet me with open arms, cut me a check on the spot–or get me cash if I preferred—take the painting, and that would be the end of it. Five minutes in and out."

"Will you do it that way?"

"Well, of course not. It doesn't hurt to take some minor precautions. I must say I've learned some valuable lessons from you and all your skull-and-dagger stuff."

I removed the blanket from the painting and watched Hadaad stare at the picture. First he frowned. Was he going to deny it? I wondered. Maybe make-believe to drive my fee down?

While he stared, another horrible thought struck me. He probably didn't know what it looked like. He wasn't with d'Lacy when he picked it up and packed it. So what would he do? Bluff his way out? Deny this was the picture, or admit he didn't know?

I showed the two photographs, the one of the good forgery—this painting—and the one of the substituted forgery, and for the tape recording I called them just that. He didn't argue.

"Well, I guess this is it," he said. "Looks like it anyway—but I still think another forgery could be made."

"Yes, doubtless," I said. "A dozen of them, given the time and the money and access to Albert Durant."

He seemed to feel his all-reaching power was being challenged. His back stiffened. "What makes you think that would be difficult?" he asked. "We got to him before."

"Yeah, but that was before the cops bottled him up."

"What? Is he in jail again?"

"Might as well be. He's under surveillance, so I wouldn't try to see him if I were you."

He frowned as you would expect him to when anyone tried to tell him what to do. "How am I going to know this is the right painting?"

"Why would I pass on to you a second forgery? What would be the point?"

"Maybe to get to the insurance company before I did."

"But if I wanted to go to the insurance company and make double or triple my fee, why would I bother to offer it to you at all?"

"Well," he said, pondering that logic, "I just don't want to be conned."

Cons never do, I thought.

"But it's up to you," I said. "You know how conscientious I am about my work. You recommended me for the job in the first place. It's because I'm conscientious that I am offering the work to you first. If you decide you don't want it for any reason, no problem. No hard feelings with me. I'll peddle it to Lloyd's of London for twenty percent of their potential loss. That's over three million. You decide."

"Let me make some calls."

"No. Now or never." I was really tightening the nails.

He stared at me, his most hateful, penetrating stare. He held my eyes in that hammerlock gaze and I'm so proud to say I just stared back without flinching. I can't possibly estimate how long we stayed like that; I know it seemed like two weeks at the time, but it was probably more like two minutes. He was the first to break concentration. Ha! He looked again at the picture.

"Okay," he said, "you give me a signed statement that this is the genuine article and I'll take it—give you your check."

"Nice try," I said. "Number one, we both know this is *not* the genuine article. It's *not* a Monet, but a clever forgery."

"All right, what *will* you sign?"

"I'll sign a statement that I bought this painting from Albert Durant. That he still claims it is a Monet original. That I had no other paintings made, to look like this or anything else. I believe this to be the same painting Franklin d'Lacy loaded in the crate for shipment to LAMMA. Further, if you or anyone else can demonstrate that is not so–that this is not the painting in question, the one you seek—then I'll refund the fee."

"Ha!" he shot from the gunwales. "You'll be long gone."

I looked him in the eye. "Really, Mr. Hadaad," I said, "you can't be serious. We both know this is the painting you bought and sold from yourself to yourself. There was a sham where you fleeced the Los Angeles Museum of eight million of their funds. You got a nice tax break for your 'donation' of the other eight million. Thus, you and d'Lacy and that poor sap Moran, who did all the dirty work, cut up the eight million from LAMMA, and you pocketed your eight million, plus you collected another mil on Moran's note."

He turned suspicious.

"I don't like people snooping into my affairs," he said.

I stared at him another painful moment. I pursed my lips, licked them and said, "Okay, I don't blame you. I'll keep the picture. You keep the check."

I had only started to pick it up and rewrap it when he stopped me by sliding his arm between me and the picture. "No, wait," he said, "I'll take it."

And he handed me the check.

I almost fainted.

I met the guy with the suitcase outside and detached and gave him my recording device. He was paying me some kind of compliment, but I didn't want to hang around there any longer than I had to. I wanted to get that check to the bank, to enjoy my freedom, and get clear of Hadaad.

The Interpol troops were going to keep him under twenty-four-hour surveillance until he tried to sell the painting to Lloyd's of London. His telephone was bugged, his room was bugged, and an electronic tracking device was inserted in the frame of the painting. In case his tail lost him, they could always find the picture.

Then Jane came out and gave me a big kiss. "We'll keep in touch," she said.

I went whistling all the way to the nearest bank, just down the block.

A pleasant young man said he would be happy to assist me in opening an account.

When he looked at the check, his Adam's apple hit the ceiling. When it settled down, he said, "This is a rather large check, Mr. Yates."

"Yes." I was smiling like one of those Worcestershire cats when I said, "Better too large than too small."

He smiled and indicated that was sound reasoning on my part. "May I see your passport, Mr. Yates?"

I took it out of my jacket pocket and handed it to him. He perused the title page. "Hm," he said, "looks like you all right, but it says your name is Malvin Stark. Who is Gil Yates?"

"Oh, that's me. That's the name I work under. I'm a detective," I said, starting to perspire. "Jane Eaton of Interpol can vouch for me," I added with a gratuitous emphasis.

"Yes," he said, "I've no doubt she can. Could you wait just a minute, sir?" he said, rising.

"Sure."

He went to the inner sanctum and returned forty days and forty nights later, during which time I had ample opportunity to chastise myself for accepting the check made out to my alias. But I wasn't about to tell Michael Hadaad my real name. I got a letter from him before, but this time, with the rush, with being in jail, with having to compromise on Hadaad for expediency, I flunked. My hope was Jane would come to my rescue.

I had convinced myself that she would, when I saw the young man striding back toward me with a white-maned gent with spats. Biggest mistake the U.S. of A. ever made, giving up spats.

"Mr., ah, Stark," the elderly gent began, "I'm Wolfgang Lindler, the bank manager. I'm afraid we have a problem."

"I can explain it all. But perhaps you would feel better if I brought Jane Eaton from Interpol in to explain it all to you."

"I'm sure I should be delighted to meet her," Wolfie said, "but I'm afraid our problem goes beyond your name."

"Oh?"

"Yes, you see, this million-dollar check is drawn on a nonexistent bank."

"What?" I sputtered, my heart rolling on the floor. "You mean the bank closed?"

"No, sir, I mean there is no such bank. It is a fiction." He tried several approaches in the hope one would hit home.

They all hit home. Hard. "How, well, but, how, I mean, how could he do that?"

"Looks to me like he just took a computer graphics program and made himself a check."

Just like d'Lacy's phony escrow company. Well, I always said, birds of a feather are very much prone to fly in packs.

216

From the Zurich airport I called Sarah. She was just as pleasant and cheerful as always. I asked her to mail me the stuff I left at her place. Then I thanked her for her invaluable help.

"It all went well then, did it?" she asked.

"All but my fee. He gave me a phony check."

"Oh, no!" she said. "Rum luck. Well, I've got a live one in back, got to run. Do keep in touch," she said, and hung up. No tears. No recriminations: The modern world. The one I missed out on.

My plane was delayed for some reason, I didn't want to know why. What good would it do to find out some dirty little screw was missing, the absence in flight of which would send us all hurtling to eternity? Would it hurt? I wondered. Then they loaded us in the plane like cattle and let us sit there for another hour, just to be sure we all had time to build up enough anxiety to see us through the trip. It was the airline's way of lobotomizing its passengers.

But, frankly, I was too bummed out by my circumstances to spend much time worrying about the plane crashing. I was so low I would almost have welcomed it. I had heretofore thought of suicide as a coward's cop-out; now I realized there were times when copping out could come in handy.

I used to love to look at the stewardesses on a plane. But now they were hiring men to do that feminine job. The women, I suppose, were trying to prove something by digging sewer lines and climbing telephone poles. The view from an airplane aisle seat used to be reliable; now it is intermittent at best.

It was one of the females on the mike, thanking us for our patience and offering us free booze as compensation. Since I don't drink booze, it didn't seem like compensation to me. As for patience, I ordinarily didn't have *any*, but now I wasn't that anxious to return to Tyranny Rex and Daddybucks. I did want to get back to my palms, of course, they would offer solace. But most of all, I didn't want to get any further from the Sarah/Jane axis. I was sure that once out of their sight, I was out of their minds, but hope does spring paternal in the human beast.

After the captain told us how sorry he was about the delay, and what good sports we were being, I got to thinking maybe I was too good a sport about my fees.

In the heat of my first case, I had spontaneously blurted that I didn't charge for expenses—that was tacky—and no thousand dollars a day—that was for small-timers. Now I had received a good lesson on the pratfalls of contingency work. If I was going to pursue this folly, I would just have to realize I wouldn't always get paid. It might even add to the adventure. On the other hand, I can't eat—or fertilize my palms—on adventure.

But somehow I would have to tighten up the operation so when *I earned* my fee (like this time) I would *get* my fee (*not* like this time).

Perhaps that was the biggest blow to my ego—not getting the money. It was the celery on the end of the stick, and when I'd finally earned it, it was snatched away from me. Sure, there is satisfaction in accomplishing your goal, but if you don't get paid...

Oh, I know all those homilies about money being the tuber of all evil, but just thinking about all this lark had cost me was sending me to the doldrums again.

Then I thought of Sarah and Jane, and I realized the case had definite positive aspects. My spirits rose.

But just as quickly, I realized I would probably never see either of them again and it was back to the doldrums for me.

Given all the time to think while waiting for this tub to take off, I speculated on what would become of my colleagues, clients and adversaries as a result of my involvement in the con caper, or independent of it. Franklin d'Lacy, I decided, would be removed from his directorship by the board of LAMMA and indicted for conspiracy to commit fraud, be convicted and live out his life in disgrace. Hadaad would be convicted and jailed and, as part of his sentence, would be barred from participating in the art market. Poor

Jacques Moran would get control of his gallery back and thrive in a new market boom.

What actually happened was quite different: Franklin d'Lacy resigned from the board, citing his uncontrollable urge to turn to creative endeavors at this crucial time in his life. He wrote a novel, which touched the *New York Times* Best Seller list for a few weeks, and edited a magazine called *Fine Arts Today*, and made quite a success of it for a few years, until he had a falling-out with his publisher over something so trivial it has been forgotten. He was never indicted. His board chose to bury the unpleasantness rather than flaunt the dirty sheets in public.

Michael Hadaad entered a plea-bargain, which did get him out of Moran's hair and forbad him from dealing in the art market. It was the only thing I was right about. Hadaad paid a hefty fine, which he would hardly miss, and was set up for one thousand hours of community service, which he spent giving stock-market tips to prison inmates.

Jacques Moran, perhaps the most innocent, suffered the worst fate. Shortly after Hadaad's plea-bargain, cousin dragon lady told Moran they had hundreds of thousands in debts, and if he couldn't pay them, she would take over his gallery. The case dragged through the courts, Moran had a nervous breakdown and is spending his autumn years in a vegetative state. The dragon lady is running the gallery, which I plan to firebomb the next time I'm in London.

I did gain a new perspective from my experience. The soft spot I had in my heart for con men has healed over with thick calluses.

There had been so many buck-up messages over the plane intercom, and so deep was my reverie, I almost didn't hear my name called out.

"Will passenger Gil Yates make himself known to the flight attendant, please?"

Oh, geez, I thought at once, they're going to throw me in the slammer after all. So I didn't wish to "make myself known." I reasoned, irrationally, if I didn't expose myself, the door might shut out the cops, and we'd be on our way.

But the voice persisted with the identical announcement, and I realized if it *was* the cops, the plane wouldn't take off until they were satisfied.

Meekly I lifted my paw.

"Oh, there you are." It was a sunny-faced blond who came toward me, clutching an envelope in her hand.

"There you are, you rascal, you," she said, leaning over to put me in delightful proximity to her upper-body charms. She patted my shoulder after she dropped the envelope in my lap. Then she winked at me as though we shared some sensual secret.

Watching her dance back toward the front of the plane, the aisle at my eye level was finally rewarding. I hadn't seen this attendant before, but the flight was definitely looking up.

I didn't open the envelope right away. I wanted to savor the messenger before I got to the message, lest the missive break the spell.

But I couldn't wait long before I tore into the pale powder-blue envelope that smelled of someone's perfume. I was hoping it wasn't a summons to return, but then I realized that would not have been handled so cavalierly—and the envelope wouldn't smell of perfume.

> *Dear Gil:*
>
> > *The sexiest guy in the universe. Sarah and Jane are missing you already. I had a pow wow with the captain about how much you helped us—and how you were defrauded of your fee. At first he said that was not his problem, but I used ALL the powers of my persuasion and he saw the sweet reason behind my proposition. So enclosed please find the fruits of your labours, as well as mine. The amount may not cover all your costs, but it is the maximum we are authorised to give, and I hope you'll find it better than a kick in the pants. But, then, I suppose that depends on who is doing the kicking.*
> >
> > *All our best wishes that you may have*

the sweetest dreams—of us, of course.
Our love,
Sarah and Jane

I looked back in the envelope which had lain on my lap. Sure enough, there was a check. It was for ten thousand American dollars.

I sank back in my ratty tourist seat and a tingly feeling of well-being washed over me. I felt cleansed of Michael Hadaad and Franklin d'Lacy and bonded forever to Sarah and Jane. It was a dream I never wanted to wake from. Then, without another thought to my palm-and-cycad collection in Torrance, California, I rose from my seat like a phoenix. I was going to get off the plane. Life had never been better and I would be a fool to leave this paradise behind.

I was only a few rows from the front when I realized the good-looking attendant who brought me the life-changing envelope was signaling frantically to me. She was strapped in a jump seat facing me. What was her problem? She was waving a hand at me. "Sir, return to your seat, please," she said, "we are taking off."

I hustled back to my seat, strapped myself in and began to work up to my customary terror. What if there was another rusty nut in the engine? One they hadn't found. What then?

My fear of flying was obliterating my memories of Sarah and Jane. I must have been back to normal. Well, I reasoned, with ten grand, I could come back and see them sometime. I was not, I had to admit, ready to cut my cord to my palms.

After landing in Los Angeles, I cleared customs with my two Durant original oils, which I valued at two hundred dollars each, keeping me within my allowance. The customs inspector glanced at them and didn't seem to feel I had been undervaluing them.

"What did you pay for these?" he asked.

When I told him the story of buying three for twenty-one hundred but having to leave the sixteen-million one behind, his wary eyes told me he had had much too hard a day to cope with another nut, so with that feeling of weariness, coupled with his sincere belief that even at two hundred dollars each I might have overpaid, he waved me through.

I never get stopped at customs. That is one of the benefits of looking like a wimp. Tyranny Rex always gets stopped. Are there any better judges of character than customs agents?

The next thing I knew, I found myself dead tired at the curb. I went back to call Tyranny Rex, but only got her answering machine. I didn't leave a message. I took the shuttle bus instead of a cab to save the twenty bucks. I got to ride around the airport twice and go along while two other travelers were deposited on their doorsteps.

When I arrived home, I dropped my stuff on the front steps and paid a visit to my remaining love—my palm garden.

I was gone less than two weeks in all, but I could see some new growth. Especially on the weeds.

I let myself in the front door, after ascertaining that the house next door was still for sale. Under the circumstances, I wouldn't be buying it *or* the twenty-five-thousand-dollar palm tree.

Tyranny was working away in her garage glass-blowing lair, her oversized goggles covering her round face. When she finished the piece she was shaping, she threw up the goggles and said, "Hi, Malvin, how was the trip?"

"Okay," I said.

"Look here," Tyranny Rex said, holding up a mélange of birds in flight, the wing of one attached to the wing of another—all at a forty-five-degree angle so the lowest wing touched the pedestal. It really was one of her nicer pieces.

"Like it?" she asked.

"Yes," I said.

"I call it 'Birds of a Feather.'"